DR. HART'S ROMANCE REMATCH

DEANNE ANDERS

MEDICAL ROMANCE

If you purchased this book without a cover you should be aware that this book is stolen property. It was reported as "unsold and destroyed" to the publisher, and neither the author nor the publisher has received any payment for this "stripped book."

Recycling programs for this product may not exist in your area

ISBN-13: 978-1-335-99376-2

Dr. Hart's Romance Rematch

Copyright © 2026 by Denise Chavers

All rights reserved. No part of this book may be used or reproduced in any manner whatsoever without written permission.

Without limiting the exclusive rights of any author, contributor or the publisher of this publication, any unauthorized use of this publication to train generative artificial intelligence (AI) technologies is expressly prohibited. Harlequin also exercises their rights under Article 4(3) of the Digital Single Market Directive 2019/790 and expressly reserves this publication from the text and data mining exception.

This is a work of fiction. Names, characters, places and incidents are either the product of the author's imagination or are used fictitiously. Any resemblance to actual persons, living or dead, businesses, companies, events or locales is entirely coincidental.

For questions and comments about the quality of this book, please contact us at CustomerService@Harlequin.com.

TM and ® are trademarks of Harlequin Enterprises ULC.

Harlequin Enterprises ULC
22 Adelaide St. West, 41st Floor
Toronto, Ontario M5H 4E3, Canada
www.Harlequin.com

HarperCollins Publishers
Macken House, 39/40 Mayor Street Upper
Dublin 1, D01 C9W8, Ireland
www.HarperCollins.com

Printed in U.S.A.

1 2 3 4 5 6 7 8 9 10 HDC 28 27 26 25

Sunshine State Surgeons

*Welcome to sunny Silver Sands in Florida,
where the surgeons are friendly, the shrimp is fresh,
and the sand is sugar white!*

The Hart brothers always dreamed big. But after swapping their football dreams for the heart racing world of medicine, Hart's Sports Medicine Institute is where they'll come face-to-face with their real matches!

Orthopedic Surgeon Michael Hart gets more than he bargained for when nurse Devon Navarro, the unforgettable crush he once shared a sizzling summer romance with, catapults back into his life—widowed with her young son. It's obvious their electric chemistry has only intensified, but can Michael forgive the life-changing secret Devon's kept from him?

Find out in...

Dr. Hart's Romance Rematch

Available now!

And don't miss

Matthew and Rachael's story

Coming soon!

Dear Reader,

People say that Florida only has two seasons, one being the wet season and the other being the dry season. But if you live in the Florida Panhandle, you know they're wrong. There are really three seasons. The dry season, the wet season, and then there is my favorite season, football season.

With that in mind, it only seemed right that I create a small beach town in the Florida Panhandle much like the one where I lived for many years before moving to the country. A quiet place where a football-loving doctor, one whose own professional football dreams had been destroyed, could build an orthopedic surgical center to help elite athletes and weekend warriors recover from their injuries, as well as a family-friendly town where a single mother could make a home with her son.

So welcome to Silver Sands, where the people are friendly, the shrimp is fresh, and the sand is sugar white. I hope you enjoy Michael and Devon's story as secrets are revealed, hearts are mended, and both Michael and Devon find the home that they both deserve.

Best wishes,

Deanne

P.S. Roll Tide (IYKYK)

Deanne Anders was reading romance while her friends were still reading Nancy Drew, and she knew she'd hit the jackpot when she found a shelf of Harlequin Presents books in her local library. Years later she discovered the fun of writing her own. Deanne lives in Florida with her husband and their spoiled Pomeranian. During the day she works as a nursing supervisor. With her love of everything medical and romance, writing for Harlequin Medical Romance is a dream come true.

Books by Deanne Anders

Harlequin Medical Romance

The Surgeon's Baby Bombshell
Stolen Kiss with the Single Mom
Sarah and the Single Dad
The Neurosurgeon's Unexpected Family
December Reunion in Central Park
Florida Fling with the Single Dad
Pregnant with the Secret Prince's Babies
Flight Nurse's Florida Fairy Tale
Festive Reunion with the Doctor

Boston Christmas Miracles

A Surgeon's Christmas Baby

Nashville Midwives

Unbuttoning the Bachelor Doc
The Rebel Doctor's Secret Child
Single Dad's Fake Fiancée

Visit the Author Profile page at Harlequin.com.

This book is dedicated to the physical therapy staff at the Andrews Institute Rehabilitation center located in Jay, Florida. My sincere thanks for all your patience and kindness.

CHAPTER ONE

Not for the first time, RN Devon Campbell questioned her decision to interview for the position of manager of surgical services at the Hart Sports Institute. As the pounding of her heart matched the clicking of her heels, she reluctantly followed the HR manager down the hallway to a suite of exam rooms. There was no doubt that she needed this job. And it was perfect for her. Since graduating from nursing school, she'd had experience in both the operating room as a circulator and as an assistant, along with experience in presurgery and recovery. This surgical center had only been open for a few months and she'd researched it enough to know that it showed all the signs of becoming a world-class orthopedics center with many well-known athletes already giving it rave reviews. Being able to be a part of the foundation of an institution like this would be very rewarding.

Also, the position of manager would give her

not only the financial security she needed, but also the flexibility to be there for her seven-year-old son, something she hadn't had at her last surgical job with its twelve-hour shifts and on-call nights. The long hours and childcare were why, after the death of her husband, Zachary, she'd had no choice but to resign from her position. Then there had been the move from California, where her husband had been stationed in the navy. While she had been excited to move back to Florida and the home in the little beach town of Silver Sands that she'd inherited from her grandmother, the closest hospitals were thirty minutes away and the commute wasn't something she'd wanted to make. She knew she could sell her grandmother's home and move closer to the city, but the last year had been hard, and being in the place where she had grown up made her feel less alone. She wanted this job. She needed this job. Shalonda, the HR manager, had all but said she would be offered the position when they'd talked on the phone.

Yes, the job was perfect in every way. If only that was the real reason she was there. Her heart sank at the thought.

They turned a corner and the real reason she was determined to get this job stood in front of them. Michael Hart, former professional football star and now orthopedic surgeon and founder of the Hart Sports Institute, dressed in a tailored suit that Devon knew had cost more than her monthly food budget, was heading down the hall toward them. At six and a half feet tall, he'd lost none of the muscular build he'd had when he was plowing through a line of defenders during one of the quarterback-sneak plays for which he had once been so renowned.

As he looked up from the clipboard in his hand, Devon's steps slowed. Unfortunately, the beat of her heart was paying no attention, and chose to speed up as if she was running a marathon instead. It was the eyes. Those beautiful pale green eyes that had always made her react this way. She would have thought that she would be used to them after seeing them every time she looked at her son.

"Dr. Hart, do you have a moment?" Shalonda asked as they stopped in front of him. "I wanted to introduce the applicant for the surgical services manager that I told you about, Devon Campbell."

Devon held her breath as Michael looked over at her. This was it. The moment she'd dreaded. Time stood still for a moment, and at first she thought he didn't recognize her. Was that really possible? After all, it had been over eight years since the last time he'd seen her. She was no longer the young, innocent college student she'd been back then. Surprisingly, the thought of him not recognizing her hurt. But why? She'd gotten over her childish crush years ago.

Then she saw something in those eyes of his change and the hurt was replaced with the fear of remembering the promise she'd made to Zach before he had died and the reason she had come home to Silver Sands.

"Sunshine?" he asked, his eyes widening and the firm line of his lips beginning to turn up in a smile.

Sunshine. For a moment the nickname made her smile. No one had called her Sunshine in years. It was a name her grandmother had called her, and later a few childhood friends. It brought back memories of lazy days on the beach after all her chores were done. The sand, the sun, and the warm emerald gulf waters had been her playground then. It had been a long time since she'd been that girl. She could barely even remember her.

"Hi, Mickey," she said, for a moment letting happier memories replace all of her fear of this meeting. She remembered that crooked smile of his that he'd used to charm her grandmother into baking his favorite chocolate chip cookies.

She remembered the way his eyes would light up when the two of them stood on his balcony and spotted a herd of dolphins playing off the shore. And she remembered the way his lips had felt on hers, gentle and sweet, the first time he'd kissed her.

Her memories screeched to a halt and her body went rigid. It wasn't just her grandmother who this man had been able to charm. She'd been a victim of his charm one too many times. Not that she could blame him for either occasion, as the first had been on the night he'd lost his parents and the second time had led to her getting pregnant with her son, when she'd been only too willing to fall for the charming man he'd become.

"So you've moved back home? Last I heard, your husband was stationed in California," he said as he studied her with an intensity that made her want to squirm.

But then, Michael Hart had always been intense about everything in his life. It was how he'd made it to the NFL and how after the injury that had ended his football career he'd pivoted into the medical field.

It didn't surprise her that he knew about her marriage. Silver Sands was a small beach town mostly made up of long-term residents, and her grandmother had been a large part of the community until she'd passed away. What was surprising was that he hadn't heard the latest news about her life. "My husband passed away last year."

"I'm so sorry," he said. There was shock, then sympathy in his eyes. "I didn't know. Have you moved into your grandmother's house? I know it's been empty for quite a while."

"It's home," she said, knowing that he would understand. He'd known her grandmother and, like the rest of the town, he knew that the only real home Devon had ever had as a child had been that little cottage across from the beach.

A nurse stepped out of one of the exam rooms and smiled at the three of them. "I'm going to put in an order for Ms. Hughes's pre-op lab work and I was about to go over the postsurgery instructions. Is there anything else you need?"

"No, thank you, Jesse. I think we have everything covered. I went over the consent and I just put it on the chart. Let me know if she has any more questions," Michael said. The woman nodded, then returned to the patient's exam room. "Why don't you tell me what makes you right for this job, Devon?"

The change in subject stunned her for a moment, then she remembered she wasn't there to reminisce about the past—she was there for an interview. "I have a bachelor degree in nursing and worked as an OR assistant while in school. I've worked as a circulator for two years. I did pre- and postsurgery at the navy hospital where we were stationed. And my last position was manager of the postanesthesia unit at the Fresno County hospital. I have a copy of my résumé if you would like to see it."

"That's not necessary. If you weren't highly qualified for this post, Shalonda wouldn't have given you an interview or brought you here to meet me. We're not a large surgical center. We specialize in orthopedic and sports medicine. While we are quickly becoming known for treating celebrity athletes, I founded the clinic to provide excellent service for not just the famous, but also for anyone suffering from an injury. We treat everyone equally and respect everyone's privacy." He began to walk down the hall and they followed him. "That being said, we also recognize that some of our patients, because of their celebrity status, require us to take more precautions to keep them protected from the media. I don't think that will be something you will have a personal problem with, but as manager it will be something that you will have to make sure is enforced in your department."

They stopped at an open door and Devon knew by the large oak desk that sat against a bank of large windows that it must be Michael's office.

"Give me a moment to make a call and I'll be right back to give you a tour of the place." Michael said.

As Michael stepped inside the office, Devon looked over at Shalonda and realized that the woman hadn't said a word since she'd introduced Devon to Michael. "My grandmother used to be Dr. Hart's parents' housekeeper here in Silver Sands, and I would tag along with her when I was a kid."

There. That sounded innocent enough. The woman didn't need to know how close she'd once been to his family. Though it didn't explain the use of each other's nicknames. Most housekeepers probably weren't friendly enough to call their employers' children by their nicknames. But then, her grandmother had been more than just a housekeeper to Michael and his brother, Matthew.

Instead of questioning Devon further, Shalonda just smiled and nodded her head. "It sounds like this has been a good surprise for Dr. Hart. The two of you should work well together."

"Do you really think he's going to offer me

the job?" She knew she should be happy that it looked like she would be getting what she wanted, yet she couldn't help but worry about how easily her memories had rushed back to a happier time, when their lives had been so tangled together.

"Well, he wants to give you a personal tour. Of course, that could be him wanting the two of you to catch up. Or it could be he wants to show off a bit. This place is spectacular," Shalonda said. "It looks to me like this will all work out great. I'm going to get back to my office. Just have Dr. Hart bring you back to me when he finishes showing you around." With that, the woman turned on her heel and left Devon standing in the hallway alone.

A few moments later, Michael came out of his office. "Sorry, I needed to check on one of my patients."

"I don't want to hold you up. I know you must be busy." And though she knew it was the perfect time for her to start executing her plan to find out if Michael was someone she wanted in her son's life, she really wasn't prepared to spend this time alone with him right now. But then, would she ever really be prepared for this?

When her husband had asked her to find Michael and explain to him about Conner, she'd been unable to refuse. Zach had been sick for almost a year by then and he'd suffered too much for Devon to deny him anything. But even now, after making the move back to Silver Sands and standing here beside Michael, she had her doubts about Zach's reasoning. She knew Zach had only been doing what he thought was best for Conner, but her husband had never experienced the teasing and embarrassment she'd suffered as a child. He didn't know what it was like to have people call his mother names. Having it come out that Conner was Michael's son instead of Zach's in her small town would cause a lot of talk. And when the parents talked, the children would hear every word. Somehow, she had to protect her son while also keeping her promise to Zach.

When she'd seen the advertisement for the surgical manager position she'd immediately come up with the idea to use the job as a way to get to know Michael again and make sure that Zach was right in thinking that it would be good for their son to have his biological father in his life. Now, she was seeing that this wasn't going to be as easy as she had thought. She couldn't seem to look at Michael without old memories returning.

"I'm really sorry to hear about your husband," Michael said again as they left his office suite and headed back down the hall toward the front entrance.

"Thank you," Devon said. It always felt awkward to have people tell her they were sorry to hear about Zach's passing, especially people who hadn't known him. "He was a good man. A wonderful husband and father, too."

"Your grandmother told me that you had a little boy," Michael said as they took another hallway, this one labeled with a Staff Only sign.

"You saw my grandmother before she passed?" Devon said, hoping Michael couldn't hear the wobble in her voice.

"I came home briefly, right before I began my residency. She was very proud of you. She showed me a picture of you and your husband and your son. She said you'd just moved to California then. You looked happy."

Devon knew the picture he was talking about. She'd found it among her grandmother's things when she'd come home for her funeral. It had been taken right after Zach had just joined the military and Conner had still been a newborn. Looking back now, her world had been perfect.

They came to a stop at a set of double doors with a sign stating that surgical attire was necessary to enter and she looked up into Michael's face. "I was very happy."

"I'm glad you were happy," Michael said, his voice low and earnest. Something passed between the two of them then as he once again studied her face. Neither one of them spoke about it—that night they'd shared—but she knew they were both thinking about it.

For a moment, they just stood there. She wasn't sure if he'd thought she'd spend her life being miserable, because he'd never called her after that night, or if he truly just meant he was glad she had been happy. Either way, she'd had enough of the past. It was time to get back to the here and now.

"So how many operating rooms do you run a day?" she asked.

"We only run four at a time right now, but we have the ability to run two more." Since they were unable to enter the ORs, as neither of them was dressed in their scrubs, Michael explained a little about the operating room setups and the staffing, then led her into the recovery room and through to the presurgery areas. As he explained the reasoning behind each department layout, she could hear the pride in his voice. It was easy to see that he had found his place in the medical world, even though it was far from the future he'd planned when they were growing up.

"This place is amazing. The technology is

first-rate and I can already tell the layout works perfectly," she said, though what she really wanted was to ask him how he'd managed to accomplish all of this in such a short time. But she couldn't let herself do that. The only way she could do what Zach had asked was to keep things strictly impersonal between her and Michael.

"I'm glad you think so," Michael said as they made their way back to the small HR department, where Shalonda was waiting for her. His phone went off and he paused to read a message before looking back up. "I'm sorry, I need to make a call so I'm going to leave you with Shalonda now. I hope you decide to join us here. As you can tell, the staff here are friendly and I think you'd be a great addition to the team."

An hour later, Devon walked out of the sleek entrance to the surgical center with an offer for a job that more than met her needs. Shalonda had told her to think about it overnight, but she'd also told her not to take too long. There were other candidates interested in the position and they wanted to get it filled as soon as possible.

Devon knew that the woman had to think she was crazy for not accepting the position immediately. After all, it was the position that she had applied for. But after seeing Michael again after all these years, she wasn't sure that she was doing the right thing.

She'd planned on basically infiltrating Michael's business to see what type of man he'd become. After seeing him and talking to him, she now felt unsure about her plan. She'd known Michael since she was thirteen. What more did she hope to learn about him?

Or was she just trying to postpone the moment that she knew would change everything? The moment she had to tell Michael that she'd had their child and never told him.

By the time she hurried home and changed her clothes, then drove to the football field, where she'd dropped off Conner that morning for camp, she was feeling better. For a moment, she'd let her guard down and forgotten the reason she was there. It wasn't to relive old times with Michael. She was there for her son.

Feeling better now, she locked her car and walked over to the bleachers, where the other parents were watching from the small stands that had been set up. She spotted Conner the moment she sat down, his hair a little more copper than her own strawberry blond, making it easy to pick him out. His face was flushed as he concentrated on the exercise they were doing. And when he looked over at the boy next to him and smiled, Devon thought her heart would explode. It had been so long since she'd seen a genuine smile on her son's face. Maybe this was a sign that coming back to her small hometown was the right thing to do. And maybe, no matter how things turned out with Michael, she'd found the perfect place for the two of them to begin to heal after losing Zach.

Michael headed to his truck at a trot. His last surgery had run longer than he had expected and then he'd gotten so caught up in all his new CEO responsibilities that now, he was going to be late. He knew he was wearing too many hats but at the moment, he had no choice. His plan to slowly open the sports institute six months ago hadn't gone quite like he'd planned. In the months leading up to its opening, he'd received so many requests from orthopedic doctors in the neighboring area to perform surgery in the new surgical center that they'd opened up with almost a full schedule. Of course, he'd vetted each surgeon. The failure of his football career just made it more important that this center was a success. He couldn't afford to have less than the best working here.

But while he was thrilled that his idea of a sports-centered surgical center had been received so well, after six months the workload was starting to get to him. He needed help. That thought reminded him that he hadn't heard from his brother in several days.

"Call Matt," he ordered his car system, then waited as the phone rang several times.

"Hey, bro. What's up?" his little brother asked. He could hear voices and the ringing of call bells in the background.

"Just checking in. What's going on there?" Michael asked. The guilt he felt about those first few years after their parents had died still haunted him. Even though it had been years since they'd repaired their relationship, he knew he had let his brother down. He'd never forget, never wanted to forget, how he'd let himself get too caught up in his own life to think about the brother he'd left behind with grandparents who'd never wanted the responsibility of caring for a teenage boy. He could take the easy way out and blame it on being busy with college and his football career, but the truth was that he'd been so self-absorbed that he hadn't given his brother's situation that much thought. Yet it had been his little brother, the one that his grandparents called irresponsible, who had been there for him after his football injury. He'd helped Michael navigate through the surgeries and the rehab that had followed, handled the media storm, and had even taken time off from his own college courses. Michael knew he wouldn't be where he was now if it hadn't been for his brother.

Michael would never be able to make up for the way he'd let Matt down, but he knew he'd never let it happen again. His brother was family. The only family he had besides his grandparents, who had only ever seen the two of them as a responsibility they didn't want.

"Nothing now. I assisted Dr. Davis with two total knee surgeries and was attending for two more. But I did get called in last night for a trauma, an open ankle fracture, which took three trauma nails to repair." His brother's voice was getting faster as he talked about the trauma case. Matt was destined to be a great orthotrauma surgeon. Pride filled Michael. They'd both lost their way for a short time, but now they were on a path that he knew would have made their parents proud.

"How's it going there? One of the other residents saw an article on the clinic that came out last week. You're getting good media coverage after that tennis star raved about how well he's doing after you did his ACL repair," Matthew said.

"First, the media coverage is great for the surgical center, which is good for both of us, not just me. That patient's recovery was remarkable and he worked hard with physical therapy to help make that happen. But I think that new femoral fixation I told you about helped with his knee stabilization, too. I'm seeing it make a big difference in the way my patients are recovering. As soon as you get here, I'm going to set you up with the vendor representative to be trained with it. Her name is Rachel and she's been extremely helpful."

"I'm looking forward to that. Anything else going on? Did you get that new surgical manager hired who was supposed to interview today?" his brother asked.

"I think so, and you're not going to believe who it is. Do you remember Devon Fitzpatrick?" Michael still couldn't believe that Devon had showed up today. He'd thought of her many times over the last few years. Like a lot of occasions in his life, things between them hadn't ended the way he would have liked.

"Sunshine? Ms. Donna's granddaughter? Of course, I remember her. It seemed she had a hard life before she came to live with her grandmother. She was so quiet when she first started coming to the house. It took months before she said more than two words to us."

"Mom said that Ms. Donna had taken custody of her because Devon's mom had let some guy move in with them and he'd get drunk and beat on the two of them."

"Yeah, that was the rumor around school, too. I never could understand why some of the kids teased her about her mom when everyone knew none of it was her fault. Remember when you threatened to beat up that kid at the high school for making fun of her? You were her hero after that. She had such a big crush on you that year, though I was definitely the best-looking of the two of us."

Michael knew his brother was teasing. It had been a joke between the two of them since they were teenagers, each one of them declaring they were the better-looking Hart brother. But Michael didn't bother to argue with him now. Scars littered his body from all the surgeries he'd had after the injuries he'd received when two defensive linemen had tackled him, crushing him into the ground and ending his pro football career. But most of his scars couldn't be seen from the outside. Even after several surgeries on his right leg and arm, his body sometimes creaked and popped, letting him know that it had been changed forever.

And as far as the crush Matt claimed Sunshine

once had on him, Michael had always thought of her as more of a little sister…until the night his parents had died. It had been that night, the night she'd found him walking on the beach, which had changed things between them. Her sitting down with him right there in the sand while he cried over the loss of his parents with her arms wrapped around him had been more than his grandparents had ever done for him. They'd talked for hours about his parents without him feeling embarrassed or judged. They'd both cried and laughed, and when the sun had just started to come up, he'd found himself kissing her. It had only been one kiss, but there had been nothing brotherly about it. Then there had been the night a few years later when they'd run into each other at the hotel in Tallahassee. That night had been an eye-opener for both of them. Seeing Devon—and he'd definitely thought of her as Devon instead of the girl he'd known as Sunshine—dressed up in a short black dress, with her strawberry blond hair up in some fancy knot on top of her head, and her long legs walking toward him in those crazy high heels, had erased all his memories of the teenage girl he'd once known.

He'd never told Matthew about that night in Tallahassee. He'd treated it as a guarded secret, one too precious to share. She'd left her number on a piece of paper that he'd found lying on top of his suitcase the next morning when he was packing to leave. He could have called her then, but he'd put it off. Something to do later, when his mind wasn't so filled with getting ready for the next game. Then he'd woken up in the hospital to find out his life had been changed forever. He could have made a comeback after the concussion he'd received, maybe even made it back after he'd recovered from the broken femur. But the complete detached bicep and rotator-cuff injury wasn't something a quarterback could bounce back from. His career had been over, and he'd been surprised to find that without football, he didn't have much of a life left.

But all of that was in the past now. The injuries had happened. He had never made that phone call. And Devon had apparently moved on quite quickly to someone else.

"Her name is Campbell now. Her husband died recently and she's moved back home to live in Ms. Donna's house."

"I hate to hear that about her husband. You know she called you the day after your injuries," Matt said, his voice becoming muffled.

"What? What did you say?" Michael asked as the background sounds on the phone went silent. Had he heard his brother right? She'd called him? "Matt? Did you say she called me?"

"Sorry," Matt said as his voice suddenly came back across the phone line, "I got on the elevator."

"Did you say that Devon called me while I was in the hospital?" Michael asked again, his voice a little more inpatient now.

"Yeah, she called several times. A lot of people called that first day, you must have gotten at least a hundred calls after people watched you get injured. It was horrific seeing you carried off the field. The media was camped outside the hospital for almost twenty-four hours. The vice president of the United States even made a call to wish you well on behalf of the president. It was crazy."

"But you said Devon called several times?" Michael asked, still surprised that he hadn't been told, though it wasn't like he'd been in any condition to take the calls those first few days. But what if he had? Would it really have made any difference?

"Yeah, after I gave your phone to your agent to handle, Devon even called my phone a couple times. Said she'd got my number from Grandpa Hart. She seemed really worried about you, but I told her you were going to be okay. It was before the team announced just how bad your injuries were, though," Matt admitted.

The announcement that he wouldn't ever be returning to his former career hadn't come until a month later. Not until after the last surgery, when the poor prognosis for a full recovery, or at least one that would make him able to return to playing football, had been determined.

"Hey, you okay?" Matt asked. "I didn't mean to bring all that up again." Matt was the only one who knew that Michael still struggled with how his dream of playing pro football had come to an end.

"No, it's fine. I was just surprised to hear Devon had called. It was nice of her to do it. I'll have to thank her." Once again, he wondered what might have happened if he'd just found time to make that one call after the night they'd shared.

"You sure?" Matt asked.

"Yes," Michael replied.

"Well, if she's as right for the manager job as you say, hire her. It would be great to work with her when I make it down there. Besides, you need the help. All you've done is work since that place opened. You have no work-life balance. It's not good for you."

"Says the brother who's working day and night

in his residency," Michael teased, his brother's words hitting a little too close to home.

"It's residency. I'm supposed to have no life. Besides, I'm the youngest brother. You're getting old, bro. It's time for you to start thinking about starting a family," Matt said. This wasn't the first time that his brother had brought up the subject of Michael settling down.

"I have a family. I have you," Michael said firmly.

"Hey, hold on a moment," Matt said. Michael could hear someone in the background talking to his brother. "Hey, Mickey, I've got to go. Patients to see and all that."

Michael told his brother goodbye and ended the call as he pulled into the community sports complex. He parked near the football field, where the town's youth played everything from Tiny-Mites to high school football, with kids starting at age five going up until graduation. The complex had needed a lot of work when he'd played there as a kid. Fortunately, he'd finally been able to get the town board to see that the community needed a safe place for the kids to enjoy sports and recreation. Now, there was talk of a public pool where people could cool off during those hot summer days and a splash pad for the younger children, too.

He'd come back to town hoping to make a difference in the community where he could. Today he was there to help his best friend, Bryan, with the summer football camp that they put on every year for the kids registered for that year's recreation teams.

After getting out of his truck, he looked up in the stands at all the eager parents, watching their offspring. He remembered looking up into those stands and seeing his own mom and dad rooting for him. He hoped every parent up there was as supportive of their kid's dreams as his parents had been.

Then he saw her. She'd changed since he'd seen her earlier that day. Now dressed in jeans and a simple white T-shirt, she looked like any other sports mom, except for that beautiful blond hair with those pale red highlights that shone bright in the sunlight. He'd always thought that was where she had gotten the nickname Sunshine. Though he knew he needed to join Bryan, he couldn't stop himself from climbing up the steps to join her on the bleachers. After seeing her today at work and then the call with his brother, he found himself wanting to know more about the woman Devon Fitzgerald had grown up to be.

"I wasn't expecting to see you again today,"

he said as he took a seat beside her. Then he realized the reason she was probably up in these stands. Devon had a son. "Is your son out there?"

For a moment, she didn't answer him—didn't even look at him as her eyes started darting around the stands as if looking for an escape. She seemed nervous. He looked around to see what had her so upset.

A whistle went off on the field, bringing their attention back to where Bryan was having all the players fall in around him. Michael looked back at Devon, who took what seemed to be a very deep breath, as if she was about to face something painful.

"Yes. My son, Conner, is out there. He's on the Mitey-Mite team," she said, still staring at where all the kids stood listening to Bryan's first-day-of-camp speech that Michael had heard so often he could almost recite it himself.

"A Mitey-Mite? That's the team Bryan and I coach." He looked over to where Devon was staring and saw a boy with hair only a shade darker than hers. Who would have ever thought that someday he would be coaching Sunshine's son?

CHAPTER TWO

DEVON COULDN'T BELIEVE IT. What were the chances that she'd come back to town and enroll her son into football only to find that his biological father was going to be the coach? She'd never even considered the possibility. Michael had once been a big-time football star, but she would have thought he'd be too busy with his new career to take time out to coach a team of seven-year-olds.

Devon stared down at the field, where she could see her son concentrating on every word his coach was saying. Conner had been fascinated with the sport since the first time Zach had taken him to a college game at their alumni weekend. Devon had gone along, thinking the five-year-old would tire and get restless during the long game. But instead, Conner had listened to his father explain everything that was happening on the field. Zach, being an IT guy, had always been interested in the strategy of the game and he'd passed his interest onto their son.

Zach had been such a good dad, so patient and caring. Yet that day she couldn't help but think about Michael and the fact that he should have been the one explaining the game he loved so much to Conner. Of course, then the guilt had set in, as it always did when she thought of Michael. But how could she be thinking about Michael being there with her son when Zach had been such a good husband and father to them both?

Yet here she was now, with Michael sitting beside her, telling her he was going to be their son's new coach.

But Conner had never been Michael's son. He was Zach's son in every way that counted. Her college friend and roommate had made that commitment to her and the child she'd carried when they'd taken their vows. And if what had grown between them hadn't been her childhood dream of love, it had been something even better. Their friendship had grown into something more real than anything she had ever known before. There never could have been a better father than Zach. Her only regret was that the two of them had never been able to have another child. But they'd both known that the radiation treatment Zach had received when he was young had meant there would no more children. And, yes, she knew that was one of the reasons Zach had been so willing to marry Devon when she'd found out that she was alone and pregnant. He'd wanted children. But that had never mattered to her. He'd been there for her when she'd needed him. Because of Zach, Conner had never had to face the childhood teasing she'd been subjected to when people had asked her where her dad was. Devon would always be thankful for that. Zach had always been there for Conner. He would always be her son's father.

It was because of Zach that she was here. He had made her promise to tell Michael about Conner. He could have been selfish and kept Conner thinking that he was their son's only father. But he hadn't wanted that. He'd wanted Conner to have someone to be there, if not to replace him, at least to fill in for him. It had been the most loving thing Devon had ever experienced. Yet here she stood, not able to do what she'd been asked to do. Not yet. Not until she was sure that Michael was someone she wanted to share her son with.

Clearing her throat, she tried to calm herself before continuing, but her emotions had been all over the place today. She needed to go home. Or maybe she just needed to change the subject.

"Thank you for showing me around the surgical center today. It was amazing."

"Opening a new surgical unit was risky and we couldn't take a chance of it not taking off. Our goal was for the Hart Sports Institute to be the premier surgical unit for professional athletes. We needed the draw that would have to help bring in the local, everyday athletes. But I also wanted to offer something for the professionals that I didn't have when I was injured," Michael said.

"What's that?" Devon asked, turning to look at him. She found herself interested in this part of him, the businessman she had never known. It was just one more piece of the puzzle that she needed to understand about him.

She'd always thought of Michael as a jock. Not that he wasn't smart. He was very intelligent. He'd never had any trouble in school. Still, she'd never imagined him going to medical school and becoming a doctor, let alone building something like the surgical center. For as long as she could remember, he'd been totally consumed with his dream of playing professional football. But now, he was not only a well-known orthopedic surgeon, but also the founder of an impressive surgical institution.

"Privacy and confidentiality, things that are

hard to find these days between the media and the internet, were two of the most important things we considered when we designed the clinic. We wanted a way for someone who preferred to keep their visit totally private to get into the clinic and out again without the public being aware. So we created areas in the hospital where we can treat our patients on a one-to-one basis when needed," Michael said.

"So that's what the private recovery rooms I saw are for," she said, thinking about the layout of the surgical center in a whole new light.

"Yes. It's also one of the reasons I knew Silver Sands was the perfect place for the clinic. We're a small town. Family-oriented. We're not full of tourists. There are no five-star restaurants or even a water park within miles. This isn't a place where you're going to have a bunch of paparazzi hanging around. While it is known that some athletes and some celebrities have used the clinic, it's unlikely that they'll run into anyone here looking for a story. It's the perfect place for someone to not only recover, but they can also go through rehab with our physical therapist, if they choose. I'm in the process of leasing a couple condos where they can have our physical therapist come to them for the first few days after recovery."

"It sounds like you've thought of everything," Devon said. She couldn't help but be impressed.

"I had a lot of time to think about it when I was in rehab myself. It was a nightmare for the first few months with the media hounding me every time I had to go out in public. It was the whole experience, the good and the bad, that made me want to go into orthopedics and open a place where professional athletes could feel at home."

He stood and waved to one of the coaches, someone Devon had known almost as long as she'd known Michael. "It looks like Bryan is ready for me. Stick around after we finish here, and we can talk more. There's something I'd like to talk to you about besides the job."

And with that, he headed down the steps and then across the field to where the young boys were waiting. She held her breath when he joined the group and she saw Conner move to the front, almost directly in front of Michael. Would he see Conner and recognize him? Would he notice the way his eyes were the same green color as his own? Would he notice that crooked smile that the two of them shared? Her brain told her he wouldn't see the similarities. But in her heart, where she'd let fear of this moment grow, she just knew that it was possible. All it would take was for him to start putting a few small things together, like Conner's age, and exactly when they'd spent their one night with one another, and he would know that Devon had kept one of the biggest secrets in her life from him.

She knew that she'd need to tell him, but she couldn't bring herself to do it. Not yet. Not until she was absolutely sure that her son wouldn't be hurt.

It wasn't that she thought Michael would ever physically harm Conner. Michael was nothing like the men her mother used to move in with them. He'd never think that it was okay to backhand a child because they were in their way, nor would he ever lock a child in their room for hours without food. It wasn't the physical abuse she was afraid of. Instead, it was the emotional trauma that could come from this situation. The kind her mother had inflicted when she'd abandoned Devon for days without calling, never thinking about how that made Devon feel unloved and unwanted. Would Michael want to know Conner, or would it make her son feel rejected if he didn't?

Besides, what was the hurry? Maybe having Michael coaching Conner's team was a great opportunity for her to see how he and her son got along together.

And what could it be that he wanted to talk to her about besides the job? Was it about that night they'd spent together? It could be considered an uncomfortable situation between the two of them if she went to work for him. But more than likely it was so deep in his past that he wouldn't even be thinking about that now, let alone bother to mention it. Would he? And if so, what would she say to him?

One-night stands were probably common for someone like Michael, but her? She'd only had the one, and to her it hadn't been as much a one-night stand as it had been one night that she had been waiting for since she was sixteen and had lost her heart to the first boy who had kissed her. Now, she realized that the first kiss they'd shared had been the action of a young boy reaching out for comfort. He'd just found out his parents had been killed in a car crash and they'd spent the night grieving together. But she'd been too young to understand that then. After that night, she'd believed that at some point Michael would see that the two of them were meant for each other. But after he'd gone to college and she'd never heard from him, she'd accepted that it hadn't meant as much to him as it had to her.

That was until the night they'd run into each other in the foyer of that hotel in Tallahassee. It wasn't like she'd gone to that hotel expecting to see him. They had both been a long way from home, her attending college there and him only in town to give a speech. It had seemed like fate had set everything up to finally bring the two of them together. It had only been after Michael had fallen asleep without one word of love or even a mention of seeing her again that the doubts had begun to form in her mind.

She'd left her phone number in the hotel so that he could call her, making it plain that she was interested in more than just that one night. She'd been a naive fool to think that Michael had intended for their encounter to become anything more.

Later, she'd spent hours searching for articles on Michael as she'd tried to figure out if he was really the man she thought she knew or if he had become someone else. Someone who would never give her another thought. She'd found several articles mentioning parties he'd attended and pictures of the women he'd escorted to them. Beautiful, sophisticated women who would not have a problem spending the night with a man without their heart being involved. She'd decided then and there that wasn't the kind of woman she wanted to be. That would never be her. She'd had one night with a man she'd built up in her imagination, but the truth was she hadn't even known the man he was then. The fact that it reminded her of something her mother would have done didn't make her feel any better.

So when he didn't call her the next day, she'd forced herself to accept she'd made a mistake in letting her heart get involved so easily and promised herself she'd never do that again. Even after she found out about his injury, she'd called him multiple times. Yet he'd never reached out to her. Then, three weeks later, there was a surprise. One that came with a test and two pink lines.

A whistle blew and she realized she'd been so lost in her thoughts that she hadn't even noticed the coaches were winding down that day's camp. She stood and waited for Conner to gather his shoulder pads and water bottle, then she saw Michael headed back her way. And right behind him was her son.

After remembering how she'd felt that day, sitting all alone on the floor of her dorm bathroom holding that pregnancy test, she wanted to run and grab Conner, then rush the two of them out to her car before Michael made it to her. She never wanted her son to feel as abandoned as she had felt that day. "Of course, that wouldn't look suspicious at all," she muttered as she forced herself to slow down. She made herself take careful steps down the bleachers and then met the two of them with a smile that she was sure was too bright.

"I saw that catch you made. Way to go, buddy," she said as she stepped around Michael and took her son's water bottle, holding it tight against her chest as if it was armor or, even better, a weapon. This was the moment she'd dreaded. The moment her son and Michael would first meet. Maybe it was better that it happen now, when they were surrounded by all the other parents and kids rushing around them. Maybe it was best to get it over with.

So before she let her nerves get the best of her and she did something crazy, like bolt off the field dragging her son behind her, she turned to Michael. "Mickey, this is my son, Conner."

"Mom, his name isn't Mickey—it's Michael Hart. You know, number sixteen," Conner said in a too-loud whisper to Devon then pointed to where there was a *16* posted on the back fence behind a goalpost. Devon remembered when she'd first seen the sign designating the number for their hometown football hero after Michael had led his team to the college football playoffs.

"But your mom has known me for a long time, so she calls me the name my parents and her grandmother used to call me," Michael said as he stretched out his hand to Conner.

As Conner reached out and shook Michael's hand, Devon held her breath. She'd never imagined this moment would ever happen. But Zach's death and her promise to him had changed everything.

"Really? You know my mom?" Conner said, looking up at Michael with eyes as wide as saucers.

"I do. We grew up together right her in Silver Sands. I played ball on this field, just like you will," Michael said, then looked over at her. "And I'm hoping your mom is going to work with me."

Conner looked over at Devon then, and studied her like he'd never seen her before. "You're going to help the coach with our team?"

Before she could answer her son, Michael's arm came around Conner's shoulders. "I just coach part of the time. I gave up football and became a doctor. I hear your mom is a good nurse so I'm hoping she'll come work with me where I do surgery."

"Why did you want to give up football? My dad said that the football players make lots of money and they don't have to work but one day a week," Conner said, his face so earnest as he insulted athletes around the world without even knowing it. "Didn't you want to make lots of money?"

"I think we've taken up enough of the coach's time for now," Devon said, taking her son's hand and pulling him beside her before turning back to Michael. "I'm sorry. He's at the age where he never runs out of questions."

"Well, of course he asks questions. If he doesn't ask he'll never know the answer. Right, Conner?" Michael said as Bryan walked up behind him and Devon finally saw her chance to escape.

She had just turned toward the parking lot when she heard Bryan call out to her. "Devon, are you meeting us at the Pizza Shack? Most of the boys are going."

She pretended she didn't hear him, but Conner had heard the word *pizza* and dug his heels into the ground. "Mom, can we go? Can we? You like pizza and this way you won't have to cook supper."

Devon looked down at her son's face and felt all her fears melt away. Since they'd lost Zach, Conner had been just as lost as she had been. He'd had some friends, both from his school and families of some military friends of Devon and Zach's, but he'd insisted on staying close to her whenever possible. He'd turned down sleepovers and playdates each time he'd been invited. Devon had even considered taking him to a therapist until she'd realized that it wasn't really depression as much as Conner didn't want to leave her alone. It was her depression that he was responding to. Her withdrawal from her own friends that caused him to want to stay close by her side. So instead of Conner being taken to a therapist, it had been her who had sought one out.

But here was Conner wanting to be a part of something. She'd hoped that once they'd gotten settled in town and he began to meet new people that this would happen. If she said no now, he might not want to go next time. She knew she had to set an example for him and also help him start flying on his own again. And wasn't this the perfect opportunity for that? In a town this size, the boys on his team would also be the boys in his school classes from now until graduation.

So although she wanted nothing more than to put some miles between her and Michael right now, she turned to her son and nodded her head, then turned to where Bryan and Michael stood waiting for her answer. "Pizza sounds good. We'd love to go."

"Thanks, Mom," her son said with a smile,

"and don't worry. I still have some of my birthday money so I can pay for it."

Devon felt her face go red, but she didn't say anything, knowing that her denying that she needed her son's money just to buy a pizza would make it look even worse. Her son had always been too attentive for his age, constantly asking questions about anything he didn't understand. And after a few times of her telling him that they couldn't buy some luxuries, like a new game for his gaming system or the fancy tennis shoes he'd seen on TV, she'd had to sit him down and explain that they had to be careful how they spent their money until she found a new job. Since then, he'd requested very few things from her, another reason that going out tonight would be good for him.

"We'll meet you there," she said, then took her son's hand in hers and headed to her car.

Michael waited at a table for two that had been placed close to where the team's players and their parents were sitting at several tables thrown together by their waitress. He usually avoided most of the spontaneous team outings, both because of his job and the fact that he felt like the odd one out as all the other coaches had families. He was the only coach of the Mitey-Mites team who didn't have a son playing.

But tonight, he'd changed his plans from going back to the office to finish up paperwork so that he could talk to Devon. He told himself that it was because he wanted to talk to her about the job, but he was afraid it was more than that. Ever since they'd spent that one night together, he'd often thought of her. Even when her grandmother had told him that she had married, he'd felt that things had been left unsaid between the two of them. He had told himself that it was his conscience that had bothered him all these years, after not calling her. But today, as they'd talked, he'd wondered if there was more to it than that.

So here he sat, watching the door and waiting for Devon and her son to come in. He'd seen her through the front glass windows pulling up in a little SUV more than five minutes ago, but neither she nor Conner had gotten out. From what the little boy had said, he couldn't help but wonder if she was inside the vehicle counting out her change to see if they could afford to come inside and join them.

Michael had always known that his family was well off. His father had been a successful neurosurgeon in Atlanta before he'd retired and moved his family down to the beach. His mother had done well also, working as a news anchor for one of the local television channels before he had been born. Both of his parents had been older when they'd met, his mother turning forty just after his birth. Not long after his brother had been born, the two of them had decided to retire to the beach. They'd searched for a small town where they could raise their sons and had bought a large home that was only a few feet from the warm gulf waters.

Then his parents had been killed after a car had run their vehicle off the road and into a parked car. They'd died instantly, the police officers had said, as if that would make an eighteen-year-old boy who'd just learned his parents were gone feel better. There had been a large settlement from the accident that had been put in a trust for him and his brother by his grandparents. His college had been covered with scholarships, even though he hadn't needed them, so his trust had been mostly untouched. Then he'd been drafted to play football, and he'd made enough money on media and television sponsorships, along with the money from his contract during his one year playing at a professional level, that he had more money than he would ever need in his lifetime if he handled it well.

Thinking that Devon might be sitting there

counting out change to buy a piece of pizza for her son made him feel sick to his stomach.

The door to the SUV opened and he relaxed when he saw both mom and son smiling as they walked, hand in hand, toward him. The bell over the door rang as it swung open and Devon's son pulled away from her and ran to a group of boys sitting at the end of one of the tables. When Devon looked around for a seat, he raised a hand and waved her over to him. He saw the hesitancy in her steps, but then she slowly walked over to the only empty chair on that side of the room. The one he'd so carefully saved for her.

"I was beginning to think that you weren't going to show," he said, and then wished he could take the words back, not wanting her to think he'd been sitting there worried that she didn't have the money to afford to join them.

"Sorry. I just needed to have a talk with Conner. He… I think he got the wrong idea about a few things." Her eyes didn't meet his and he could see that she was embarrassed.

He wasn't really sure what her situation was as far as her finances went, but he did know a way to help that wouldn't be embarrassing for either of them. Actually, it would help him out as much as it seemed it could help her out. "I wanted to talk to you about the job. Shalonda sent me a message saying that she had offered you the position and you were considering it. What can I do to help make up your mind?"

For a moment she looked taken back, her eyes a little wild, as if he'd cornered her. "Is it the hours? The money? I know we're a new facility without any type of financial history, but I can guarantee that we are financially stable. We are almost at capacity when it comes to our office space being rented out and our daily surgical schedules are getting filled up faster every day."

For a moment all she did was stare at him, her mouth half-open and a deep crease forming between her eyes. Then she started laughing, and both her hands came up to cover her face. He was afraid she might be crying, but when she let her hands fall, there was nothing but a broad smile on her face. "Are you trying to convince me to take a job with you because my son had some misguided belief that I couldn't afford to buy a pizza?"

"No, I mean…" He wasn't sure what to say. "No, not really. Though it did cross my mind. I had planned to talk to you about the job, anyway. That's why I had asked you to stick around after the game. I just thought…"

"You thought I was desperate for money and you wanted to help me out," she said, now sounding a little annoyed at him. "Yes, I need a job for the money, Mickey. It is why most people apply for jobs, you know. But I'm not destitute, if that was what you were thinking."

"I didn't mean to insult you." He looked around the room as if he could find some way out of the hole he'd dug for himself, because right now, she reminded him of her grandmother. If there was one thing Ms. Donna had it was a strong sense of pride.

"I really do want to hire you. I need a good manager. The one we had originally hired had to move not two months after we opened when her husband got transferred to Texas."

"Oh, I know you need me. But I'll bet you a whole pizza that you were sitting here about to offer me more money than what Shalonda and I had already discussed, just because you thought I was broke."

He didn't say anything, unable to deny that the thought had crossed his mind.

"Well, no matter what you might think, I don't need anyone's charity," she said, her deep green eyes narrowing at him.

The server, who Michael planned on giving a generous tip, picked that moment to interrupt them, taking Devon's order for a soft drink and assuring Michael that the pizza he had ordered, for the two of them, would be out momentarily. Devon tilted her head toward him and her eyebrows went up with her unspoken question.

"Yes, I ordered a pizza for both of us. The one with all the meats and vegetables that you use to love. I've also ordered for all the kids." It was definitely time for him to change the subject. He could circle back to the job after she got over being mad at him. "I spoke with Matt today. I told him you'd interviewed for the job. He was really excited to hear you had moved back to town. He said you'd called him a few times after I was injured."

"He only told you today, after all this time, that I had called you after you were hurt?" she said, then took a drink of the water that had been provided. "You didn't know I'd called?"

"No, I didn't. Don't be mad at him. Things were crazy then, with the media, my coach, my agent. I don't know what I would have done if Matt hadn't showed up to help out." It had been called "the Great Tragedy" by the media. There had been so much hype about him being the number one draft pick. Then the games that the team had won that season had just doubled the amount of press coverage he'd received. He'd felt lost during those first days, weeks, and months. It had been a lot like the loss he'd felt when his parents had been killed. He'd felt alone and vulnerable, something that a six-foot-six, two-hundred-and-thirty-pound pro quarterback could never let anyone see. But Matt, barely twenty, had plowed through all the people surrounding Michael and taken over. He was the one person who Michael had known he could trust when the pain and medication had left his grasp of his surroundings a bit tenuous.

"I'm not mad," Devon said slowly. "I'm just surprised you didn't know I'd called until now."

Their pizza came and neither of them spoke much as they ate, with just a few comments about the deliciousness of all the pizza's cheesy goodness.

Then Michael felt a tug on his shirt and looked over to see that Devon's son stood beside him. "Excuse me, Coach Hart. I just wanted you to know that I'm sorry if I said something that might have given you the—" the boy paused and took a breath "—m-press-on that my mom doesn't have any money. I didn't mean to embarrass her. She does have some money. We just have to be careful with it until she gets a job. Until then, we have to save all our money so we don't get our electricity turned off, because then I won't be able to play any of my video games."

The boy left their table then and ran back over

to join the boys from his team as they all tucked into the pizza Michael had bought. He looked over at Devon, whose mouth was open, a piece of stringy, melted cheese clinging to her lips. "I can't believe he just did that. He… I just tried to explain to him that we had to pay the bills first before we spent anything on extras. I thought he understood."

Michael couldn't help but smile. "He's a kid. Give him a break. I think it was very nice the way he was trying to help you."

"If he helps me any more I'm going to start finding casseroles at the front door." She shook her head as if she couldn't believe her child's behavior, then looked up at him. "So tell me more about this job, because it looks like I need to get one before my son has Child Services over at the house checking out my cabinets for food."

So he told her about the job, most of which he was sure Shalonda had already gone over. Then he told her about his and Matthew's dream for the place, their hopes that the surgical center could grow and provide more rehabilitation services for the community as well as professional athletes. "I don't want to make you take this job if it's not what you're looking for. It's going to take time to build the practice here, even though we're off to a great start. But if you decide you do want the job, come in Monday morning. Shalonda will do the paperwork then and you can start right away."

She nodded her head at him, but he didn't miss the fact that she didn't actually say she'd be there Monday. He wanted to ask her just what it was that was holding her back, but he didn't want to push too hard.

While they finished their pizza, Michael told her more about his and Matt's plans, and she gave him suggestions that were helpful. A few minutes later, he watched as Devon and Conner walked across the parking lot, once more hand in hand. For a moment he wondered what would have happened if he hadn't been so tied up in that dream of his to play football at the highest level. Or better yet, what would have happened if he hadn't been injured two days after the night they'd spent together? Could they have had more than just that night together? Could they have taken the friendship they'd had for years and built something more out of it? If he had called her and arranged to see her again, would the two of them perhaps even have had a family? Would it be him buckling their son or daughter into the car right now, getting ready to head home together?

He shook his head. He'd quit wondering about

what life would have been like if he hadn't been injured many years ago. What had happened between them all those years ago was in the past. Devon had gone on to marry and have a son. She had probably not given that night another thought.

But there had been those phone calls she'd made to him that left him wondering if maybe that night had meant more to her, too.

CHAPTER THREE

MONDAY MORNING, Devon made the dreaded first day of drop-off at the elementary school. As the line crept closer and closer to the front door area, where the teachers met the students and helped them onto the sidewalk, she noticed Conner squirming more and more in his seat. "What's wrong? Did we forget something?"

"No, ma'am. This school just looks different. It's kind of old and spooky. And what if I don't know anyone in my class?" Conner said as he stared out the window at the other children unloading and heading into the building.

"It's not that old. I remember when they built it."

"It's that old?" Conner asked, his wide eyes telling her that he must think of her as ancient.

"It's okay. I'm sure it's had a lot of renovations and it even has the internet now," Devon said as she eased another car length closer. "And I didn't know anyone in my class my first day of school when I moved to town. I'm going to tell you a secret. I was scared. I even tried to get my grandma to take me home."

She still remembered the look on her grandmother's face. Then Devon had explained that she wanted to go home, where her grandpa was, not to the home where her mama lived. She'd never asked to go back to live with her mother. After the constant moving in with one "uncle" after another, the security of her grandparents' home had been like heaven to her.

"But you know what? I made lots of friends that first day, and some of them are even still my friends," she said.

"Like Coach Bryan and Coach Hart?" he asked.

"Yeah, like your coaches," she said as she finally pulled up to the front door and one of the teachers, who looked familiar to her, opened the back passenger door. "Cassie? Cassie Long? Is that you?" She waved at the woman, then watched to make sure her son didn't forget anything as he climbed out.

"Sunshine? I'd heard you were back." Cassie glanced behind her at the cars that still waited in line then back to Devon. "Sorry, I can't talk now, but we need to get together soon. Maybe Friday, after this madness is over?"

"Sure. I'll send a note tomorrow with Conner so you can message me, if that's alright?" Devon said.

"Sounds great." And with that, Cassie slammed the car door shut. She didn't envy her friend for what this first day of school would bring as she waited for the line of cars in front of her to all move forward. Cassie had always wanted to be a teacher, while Devon had never been able to decide what she wanted to be when she grew up. She'd been lucky to find her way into health care after Conner was born, especially surgical services. She just hoped her friend was as happy with her choice as Devon was with hers.

Once she made it out of the school drop-off line, she headed back to the main highway that ran through town. The one where she'd have to decide whether to take the fork that led to the north of town, where Hart Sports Institute had been built, or the fork that led back to her home located along the bay side of the beach.

She'd tossed and turned every night since she'd left Michael at the Pizza Shack without giving him an answer to his job offer. She knew she wanted the job. Needed the job. Even though the school drop-off line was dreaded by most mothers, it was something she wanted to be able to do while Conner was young. If she took another surgical job she'd have to find early morning childcare, which wouldn't be easy. Besides, it had all been part of her plan to get to know Michael. So why was she not just accepting the job and getting on with it?

Maybe because it wasn't just Michael learning about Conner that was holding her back? Maybe because she feared that being around Michael again might start up all those old feelings she'd had for him when she was young?

Okay, that was ridiculous. She wasn't the naive girl she'd been when she'd had the crazy dream that Michael Hart, their high school star quarterback, and son of one of the richest families in town, would someday look at her and fall madly in love. She'd given up on that dream even before they'd run into each other in Tallahassee, the night she'd gotten pregnant. If nothing else, the love she'd found with Zach, a love that had grown from friendship and trust, had made her immune from all of those old, unrealistic feelings for Michael. She knew now that love was more than a kiss that curled her toes, or one single night of passion, however magical it had been.

After she'd tried and failed to get in touch with Michael, and then learned that she was pregnant, she'd needed Zach's friendship and support more than ever. When he'd first offered to marry her, she'd turned him down. But after Zach had confided in her about his diagnosis of cancer as a child and the fact that he would probably never be able to father a child due to the treatment he had received, she'd considered it more seriously. She'd made one last attempt that night to call Michael's brother and learned that Michael wasn't taking any phone calls. Once more, she had felt like the little girl who had been forgotten by her mother. Alone, unimportant, and doomed to repeat her mother's mistakes.

Yet the night they'd shared the pizza, Michael had acted like he had just heard about her calling him. If he was telling the truth, she couldn't hold him responsible for not talking to her. Still, he'd made no effort to call her the day after she'd left the hotel, either—and that was before his accident. Which had been a clear sign that the night hadn't meant anything to him. She'd been just another woman who had passed in and out of his life just as her mother had been in several men's lives over the years when Devon was growing up. She had made sure she'd never be that woman again. Now, she just needed to be sure Michael was no longer that same man.

And that was really the only thing that mattered now. It was Conner she needed to be concentrating on. Not Michael. Not her. Conner.

She got to the road that turned north. The surgical center had been built just a mile from there. She looked the other way, where the highway followed along the path of the intercoastal waterway and a bridge led across to the beach that was sandwiched between that and the gulf. She took a deep breath, prayed she was making the right decision, and took the road to the center.

A few moments later, she pulled up in front of the building and put her car in Park. She could sit there questioning the wisdom in taking this job, or she could open the car door and get out.

Someone rapped on the passenger window and she looked to see Michael standing beside her car. It seemed like it was time for her to tell him her decision. She unlocked the door, but before she could climb out, she found him getting in beside her. Her SUV suddenly felt like one of those crowded clown cars.

"Hi," she said, feeling more than a little self-conscious to have been caught sitting outside in her car staring into space.

Michael had always been large for his age when they were growing up. By the time he was in high school, he had stood over a head taller than everyone else in the school. But it hadn't just been his height that had made him stand out. Following his dream to play professional football had meant hours spent in the weight room. From the way he filled out the dark blue dress pants and white button-up shirt he was wearing today, it was obvious that he'd continued working out even after the injuries that had ended his football career. She knew it had to have been painful going through all of the physical therapy he'd had to do to recover from his injuries. Then to know that no matter how hard he worked he'd never be the athlete he'd once been? If nothing else, she admired that he'd picked himself up and done the work while some people would have just given up. And then to have gone further and pursued a career in medicine—that was more than anyone would have expected.

"I just thought I'd see if you were coming in," Michael said, turning in the seat toward her, his arm brushing against hers. "Is everything okay? Are you waiting for something?"

"Sure, everything's fine," she said, though she was beginning to feel a little breathless. It was as though just Michael's presence this close to her had sucked all the air out of the car.

"Look, I did a lot of thinking about you and this job this weekend," Michael said as his hand came up and rubbed his chin.

All of Devon's uncertainties about taking the job suddenly evaporated. Was he going to rescind his offer? Had he decided he didn't want to put up with her hesitancy over taking it? She knew she'd been lucky to be even considered for the job, and suddenly she realized she really wanted it. Why did she have to struggle with every decision she made after losing Zach? Always question if she was doing the right thing?

"I don't understand," she said. "Did you come out here to tell me that you'd changed your mind about offering it to me?"

"No, of course not. I'm serious when I say you are perfect for the job. Shalonda was in charge of recruitment and she offered you the job because your interview went well. I did have the final say, but I agreed with her decision. It wasn't because we have a past together. I want the right person in place for every job here. I don't really know how to explain it. It's just that having my family name on this place makes it so important for me to make it the best that it can be."

"I understand. In some ways this is a memorial to your parents. To what they meant to you." She had thought a lot of his parents, too. Not everyone would have let their housekeeper bring her granddaughter to work with her. But the Harts had welcomed her into their home just as they had her grandmother.

"You're right. To me, my whole career is a memorial to them. Even though they weren't there when my football career ended, I knew that if they had been, they would have believed in me. They'd have told me I was still capable of dreaming big and making that dream come true. They supported me no matter what. And I know I couldn't have done any of this without their belief in me, even though they're no longer here."

For a moment, Devon couldn't speak. Michael had always been passionate about his career, but to hear him give all the credit to his dead parents was so moving.

He rubbed his chin again, then placed both his hands down by his side. He turned his eyes away from her, and if she didn't know better she would have thought that the famous Michael Hart was embarrassed. "I wondered if maybe it was the past we shared that was causing you to hesitate about taking the job. I thought perhaps we needed to talk about that night, the one where we ran into each other at the hotel in Tallahassee. You know, the night we spent together."

So here it was. The talk that she had been dreading. But was this really the perfect time for her to tell him about Conner when they were just starting to get to know each other again?

Michael knew the fact that he couldn't look Devon in the eye right then was ridiculous. He shouldn't feel like a teenager trying to talk to his girl after they'd spent the night in the back seat of his dad's car. They were both adults. Maybe they had been too young when they'd spent that night together, but they'd both been plenty old enough to make an informed decision. The concussion he'd received when he'd been injured on the football field might have taken away some of his memories of the previous days, but he still remembered every single moment of the night he'd spent with Devon in minute detail. Not that he was going to tell her that. If anything, it would give her even more of a reason not to want work for him!

"No," Devon said abruptly, "we don't need to talk about that night. Not ever."

"Are you sure?" he said, glancing over at her to see her knuckles going white where she gripped the steering wheel. "It's not like we did anything wrong."

But he had done something wrong. Though he'd thought about it several times while he'd been recovering, he'd never called her. His head had been too messed up to do it. His life had changed so much that night when two three-hundred-pound defensive tackles had plowed through his offensive line and crushed him between them. He'd had no idea when he'd stepped on the field that night, surrounded by a sold-out crowd and television cameras, that he was experiencing the last moments of the life he'd spent years working so hard for. The sports announcers had all claimed that he had a wonderful, long career ahead of him and he'd believed them. Not once had he considered that his life wouldn't follow the path he'd set. But that night all his dreams had died. He'd thought for a short time that he might as well die along with those dreams. But then, with the help of his brother, he'd gotten his head on straight and realized there was far more to life than the game. Soon, he was dreaming a new dream. One that had led him back home.

Still, what if it hadn't happened? What if he'd never been injured that night? Would he have called Devon the next day? Or the next? Did it even matter now? Devon had gone on to marry and have a child. So why did he still feel like there was something unfinished between the two of them? "I still owe you an apology. I should have called you the next day."

"No, that's not necessary. It was all so long ago. I'm sure you had your reasons." Michael could hear the panic in her rising voice. Whether she wanted to admit it or not, he'd just touched on a tender subject. He wanted to push more to see where it might lead them, but he knew he couldn't, not when he could see that it was upsetting her.

"And I've already decided to take the job. I don't want you to think I don't understand what a privilege it is to be considered for a position here. The only reason I've been hesitant is that I've been trying to make the best decision for my son. I haven't been a single mom for long. Zach, my husband, and I always discussed things together."

"It sounds like the two of you were happy together," he said. He found himself becoming more and more interested in the life she'd built over the last few years. He knew losing her husband had to have been devastating because he still keenly felt the loss of his parents. Yet somehow, she'd been able to pick herself up and keep going.

Michael looked over at her and was relieved to see that Devon had relaxed some. He hadn't brought up the subject of that night to embarrass her in any way.

She looked back out the window to where they faced the front of the surgical center. He found himself wondering what was going on in her head. She always seemed to hold back all her emotions and thoughts as if she was hiding them away, not trusting either herself or him with them. He wished he knew which one it was.

"Your parents would have loved this," she said, then smiled. "They'd be so proud of you."

Michael let her change the subject. Maybe she was right and it was best that they forget the night they'd shared. "Thank you. I think so, too, though I'm sure it hasn't always been the case."

"What do you mean?" she asked, turning toward him. "Do you think they'd be upset that you didn't return to playing football? I'm sure they'd have been heartbroken for you, but they would have been more concerned about your safety."

"No, nothing like that. My parents were okay with me playing football, but they also believed in me having a backup plan. They were the ones who insisted that I got a premed degree. What I mean is the way I handled everything after their deaths. They would have expected me to take care of Matt better than I did. I failed them there." When Devon looked at him questioningly, he continued. "After they passed, I should have been there for him. I was his older brother. But, as always, I only had my mind on the ball. The football, I mean."

"Yeah, you were pretty blind to everything else when we were growing up, but I think you had to be to succeed," Devon said thoughtfully. "And I think it's amazing what you've accomplished here."

"Thanks for that," he said as his hand covered hers where it sat on the console and squeezed. "And I don't think I ever thanked you for sitting with me that night on the beach after we found out my parents had been killed. So I'm telling you now that it meant a lot to me to have someone there with me."

They sat for a moment before she pulled her hand out from under his. "I guess I need to go tell Shalonda that I'm here to fill out all those employment forms."

Not wanting to give her a chance to change her mind, he opened the car door, climbed out, and waited for Devon to join him. Then they walked into the building, where they were met by the receptionist. "Good morning, Sheila. I'd like you to meet our new surgical staff manager."

CHAPTER FOUR

BY THE MIDDLE of her second week at the Hart Sports Institute, Devon had met all the surgical staff and started shadowing them in their duties. She'd found in her last position that working side by side with her nurses and techs helped her understand exactly what they did, which in turn helped her know what they needed to do their jobs. Very few of the staff had complaints, and she found herself being impressed with not only the staff, but also the processes that Michael and his team had put into place for the safety of their patients. From what she could see, the surgical center was being highly successful in its' mission of giving the best care possible to every patient that entered there, whether it was a professional athlete who was suffering from a sports injury, or a stock boy at the grocery store.

That night as she was getting Conner ready for bed, she was feeling good about her decision to return home. She liked her job and Conner was happy with his new friends, though there were still times when he'd climb into bed with her in the middle of the night. Her therapist had told her this was probably because he had a fear of losing her like he had lost his father, which made her worry even more about what would happen if he got too attached to Michael, and Michael wasn't there for Conner when he needed him. She didn't need her therapist to tell her that it was her own childhood abandonment issues that caused her to fear this outcome for her son so strongly.

"Did you know that Coach Hart won a Claymont Trophy?" Conner asked her as he climbed into bed. "Eric says he was the most famous football player ever."

"He was pretty good," she said as she pulled the covers up over him. She didn't mention the notebook she had full of newspaper and magazine clippings of Michael's football career that she had collected from high school until the night of his injuries. She'd never even shown Zach that notebook. She knew she should have thrown it away after she got married, but something had always held her back.

"He got hurt real bad, though. Max says he had to become a doctor because he couldn't play football anymore. He must be sad that he doesn't get to play football, don't you think? Being a doctor can't be near as much fun as being a football player," Conner said, then yawned. "Daddy said that I could be a famous football player if I worked hard enough. Do you think I could ever be as good as Coach Hart?"

Devon was used to her son's insistent questioning, but this one hit a little too close to her heart. She'd never considered whether her son would follow in his biological father's footsteps. Conner had only been five when he and Zach had attended their first college football game together, and from that moment on, her son had become obsessed with it. When she'd mentioned her concerns, Zach had assured her that it was natural for him to be interested in sports. All boys liked to kick and throw balls. But growing up, Devon had seen the way Michael had been so incredibly driven by the sport. Was it possible to pass that drive and talent on to another generation?

"Mom, are you okay?" Conner asked, then yawned again.

"I think we're both tired," she said, then leaned down and kissed her son's forehead. "I love you, Conner."

"Love you, too, Mom," he said, then turned over in his bed. She stood there for a few moments until his respirations became even and she knew he was sleeping. She had no doubts that if he dreamed tonight, it would be of footballs and trophies.

She changed into her favorite oversize shirt, one of Zach's with the United States Navy's logo stamped across the chest, and settled down for the night. She started to open her laptop and review her schedule but then decided to watch some television instead. After twenty minutes, she turned the TV off. Conner's insistent talk about Michael had her mind racing. For the last few days, she'd made a point to ask the staff what they thought of the founder of the surgical center and not once had she heard someone say something negative about him. It seemed everyone, including her son, thought the man could do no wrong. Yet there had been something she had noticed. Except for his coaching the kids' team, no one knew anything about his personal life. It was like his whole life revolved around making his career and the new surgical center a success. Which made her wonder, how would he handle suddenly having a child in his life?

Finally, she went to make herself some chamomile tea, hoping that it would help settle her enough so that she could rest. When the tea was ready, she took her cup and stepped outside, onto the porch. While her grandparents' home hadn't been built on the water, being just across the road she could still hear the waves at high tide when they came crashing against the shore. She sat down into an old rocking chair where the yellow paint was beginning to peel. It was her grandmother's rocker and it made Devon feel close to her when things were quiet. She'd had many late-night conversations there on the porch. She'd shared every heartbreak with her grandma, and there had never been a secret between them, not until the day the pregnancy stick had shown two pink lines. She'd felt terrible about not telling her grandma the truth about Conner's father, but she had known it was best that she keep it between her and Zach. Back then, her grandma had recently been diagnosed with heart failure and Devon couldn't bear to disappoint her. Having Devon turn out pregnant and unmarried, like her daughter, would have broken the old woman's heart.

So instead she had shown up one weekend at the cottage and told her grandma that she and Zach were not only married, but also expecting a baby. Her grandma had been shocked, but also excited. It seemed her heart condition was worse than she'd let on to Devon and her prognosis was poor. She had admitted to Devon that she had feared she'd not live long enough to see Devon become a mother, or to hold her great-grandchild. Devon knew then that she had made the right decision when her grandmother had passed when Conner was still a toddler.

She wondered what her grandmother would think of what Devon was doing now. Knowing her grandmother, if she was there at that moment, she'd be telling Devon to stop stalling and get on with it.

A large truck passed the house then stopped and began to back up. Devon sat up, her teacup in her hand as she prepared to head inside and defend the security of her home if she needed to. Silver Sands was a peaceful little town, but after the things she'd seen in the operating room over the years, she was always aware that bad things happened no matter where anyone lived.

The car door opened just before Devon had reached for the door handle, and she recognized Michael as he climbed out of the car.

"Devon, is that you?" he asked, his voice sounding uncertain as it carried up the driveway.

"Yes, why? Is something wrong?" she asked. She sat back down in the chair and remembered that the shirt she was wearing only hit midthigh. Well, it wasn't like she had been expecting anyone this time of night.

"I didn't mean to scare you," he said as he walked up the porch steps. "I just thought I saw a ghost for a moment."

"A ghost?" she asked, noticing that he was still wearing the clothes he'd had on at Conner's practice earlier that night.

"Sorry, it was just that I used to see your grandma sitting out on that porch when I was growing up. It's natural for me to look up at the porch when I pass by." He looked down at the scarred porch floor and she would have sworn that he was embarrassed by the admission.

"I miss her, too," she said. "Even though she would say she was just a housekeeper, she was more than that to a lot of people. Everywhere I go in town people tell me how much they miss her and how much she meant to them. They share stories about her with me and I love that." As she was talking, he sat down in the rocking chair beside her.

"The whole community misses her. I think she was more family than housekeeper to the people she worked for. I know my parents felt that way. She was more of a grandparent to me and Matt than our own grandparents," Michael said.

The two of them sat in silence for a moment, both lost in memories of a woman who'd lived a simple life, but would be remembered for that very life.

A soft breeze blew across the porch and Devon reached up and brushed her hair out of her eyes. Looking up, she saw Michael studying her too intently for comfort. Unable to help herself, she turned her eyes away from his, and stared across the street, where she could see just a sliver of the gulf between two beach houses on the other side of the road. She knew it was ridiculous, but she had this crazy notion that he could see that she was keeping something from him just by looking at her. It seemed the longer she was around him, the more guilt she felt for keeping the truth about Conner from him.

"Have you been at the football field all this time?" she asked, hoping to not only change the subject, but also drown out all her confusing thoughts.

"No, I went back to my office to finish some work. It's becoming more and more clear that I need to have someone take over the administration duties. I thought when Matt came on, that between the two of us we would be able to keep control of the center. I mean, it's our place. It seems we should oversee things. But more and more it feels like I'm becoming a businessman rather than a doctor."

"For some reason I always thought you would end up a businessman, after your football career was over, of course," she said, then winced. "Sorry, that was insensitive of me."

Michael laughed, then stretched his long legs out in front of him and sighed with what sounded like relief. She wondered if just thinking about his injuries made his body remember the pain.

"It's okay. It happened," he said. "I'm not saying that I don't still miss the game or that I don't wish it hadn't happened. I do. But having everyone tiptoe around it doesn't help anyone. And coming back here and coaching the kids has helped."

"The kids love it, too. It amazes me the way you handle it, though. So many people would be bitter about having a career they'd worked so hard for taken away so quickly. But you just bounced back and now, you've made a whole new life for yourself." Devon could still remember the way the sports channels had run that career-ending play over and over again. She'd found herself glued to social media, looking for any news about Michael's recovery.

"I didn't bounce back as easily as the media seemed to imply. For the first few months, I truly believed that the doctors were wrong, and if I just worked really hard I would be back on the field by the next season. I had to come to the realization that my body would never be the same for myself. I've learned since that every athlete has to come to that realization at some point. Mine just came sooner than expected. And it was a very hard pill to swallow when I did."

He looked over at her and she could see that no matter what he said, talking about the end of his football career bothered him more than he was willing to admit. Other than the night she'd comforted him after his parents were killed, it was the first time she could ever remember seeing any sign of vulnerability in him.

He stood and turned away from her suddenly, as if he knew she had seen the pain in his eyes. "I'm keeping you up and we both have work tomorrow."

Devon stood and watched as he walked back to his car, then froze when he turned back around. "Good night, Sunshine."

"Good night, Mickey," she whispered as he drove off.

Later, as she tried to fall asleep, her thoughts kept returning to that moment of vulnerability she had seen in Michael. For as long as she could remember, he had been the town hero. Then there had been college and he'd been the star of the football team. Had he ever been allowed to be just a normal guy?

For a moment she allowed herself to imagine the two of them being just normal people. She let herself wonder what might have happened if she and Michael hadn't spent that one night together. She'd spent so much time feeling hurt that he hadn't ever tried to contact her afterward. What if she really was just a single mom with a son who had lost his father? Would things be different between them now?

"Grr," she growled, punching her pillow before turning it over to the other side. She was doing it again. Even after everything that had happened, she still appeared to have this fairytale crush on the man who'd broken her heart. The same man who'd never called her, not once but twice. She knew she couldn't really blame him for not calling her after the kiss they'd shared the night he'd lost his parents. His whole life had suddenly been turned upside down… just as it had after his football injury. But she'd truly believed that, after their night together in the hotel, she'd meant something special to him. He could have reached out to her the next day, yet he'd clearly chosen not to.

She grumbled and rolled over again. None of this reliving the past was helping. She had to separate all those memories from what was happening in the present. Right now, she was trying to build a life for her son and keep her promise to Zach. The only reason she was spending time with Michael was to determine if telling him about her son was the best thing for Conner. That was all she was doing. None of this had anything to do with all those old feelings that she was remembering now.

Feeling better, she rolled over one more time, closed her eyes, and finally drifted off to sleep.

Devon had just finished restocking the anesthesia cart in operating room three when the cell phone she'd been given for work rang. She pulled it from her scrub jacket and saw that it was the recovery unit calling. She'd just made her rounds through there an hour earlier and the nurses had all been busy. If the volume of procedures continued as they had in the two weeks she'd been there, she'd need to speak with Shalonda about hiring another nurse.

"This is Devon," she said, then listened as Carolyn, one of the newer nurses in the department, explained that she had a patient she was concerned about, but she was having a problem getting the orthopedic surgeon, Dr. Morgan, to listen to her concerns. Devon had only met this particular doctor, who specialized in shoulder injuries, one time and she hadn't been overly impressed. He seemed to be one of those surgeons who thought that when he'd finished the surgery, his job was done. From what she'd learned from the staff, he never checked on his patients after they made it to the recovery area and he was typically slow to return the nurses' calls.

"I'll be right there," she told the nurse, then locked the anesthesia cart.

As she entered the recovery room, she saw Carolyn standing by a stretcher, where a man who looked like he was in his seventies lay. It only took a minute for Devon to recognize the man as the owner of the bakery where she and her grandma had purchased donuts on Sunday mornings on their way to church. She'd only been in a couple times since she'd moved back, but Conner seemed to love those donuts as much as she had at his age.

"Mr. Waters, how are you feeling?" Devon asked as she looked at the monitors and didn't like what she saw. The man's blood pressure was extremely high at 242/112 and his heart rate was up into the 140s. Not only should the doctor have listened to the nurse when she'd called, but he also should be here already, by his patient's side.

"I've been better," the man said. "I can feel

my heart racing. I have these palpitations sometimes, but they don't last this long. And I'm a bit short of breath right now. Is this normal?"

She studied the monitor a little longer. "Mr. Waters, have you ever been diagnosed with atrial fibrillation?"

"No, I don't think so," the man said. "Is there something wrong? Dr. Morgan said I'd feel some pain after the procedure, but I wasn't expecting to feel it in my chest. It must be from that anesthesia stuff they gave me."

The man seemed to grow paler as she watched him.

"David, can you bring an EKG machine over here? We need to get a twelve lead on Mr. Waters now," Devon called to another nurse and then reached over to the oxygen meter on the wall. She increased the oxygen flow as David rushed over to them with the EKG machine and began applying the electrodes. "Carolyn, is there anything else ordered for Mr. Waters's blood pressure?" she asked quietly.

"No. I explained that to Dr. Morgan. He insisted that the problem was pain control and that I wasn't doing my job properly if his patient was in pain. Then he hung up on me. I tried to call him back, but I'm just going to voice mail now. I left a message, but he hasn't returned my call,"

Carolyn replied, equally quietly. "And the OR just called to let me know they are bringing me another patient out now."

Devon wanted to tell her nurse exactly what she thought of doctors who blamed the nurses for things beyond their control while not addressing the problem themselves, but she held her words back. "If you'll call Anesthesia and have them come assess the patient for me, I'll take over Mr. Waters while you get the new patient settled."

As Carolyn made the call, Devon reviewed the twelve lead EKG and wasn't surprised to find that Mr. Waters's heart was in an atrial fibrillation rhythm. "Have you ever been told that your heart was in an unusual rhythm? Maybe you saw a cardiologist and they told you that you had A-fib?"

"No, I've never seen a cardiologist before. My wife sees one. A nice one. But I've never had the need for one. My ticker is as good as the day I was born."

Devon didn't want to break the news to the man that his "ticker" was definitely not as good as he thought. Instead, she pulled out the phone and sent a message to Michael, letting him know that there was a problem. In a moment, the doors opened and both Michael and Dr. Smith, the anesthesiologist, walked into the unit. After Devon explained the situation, Michael pulled out his phone and called the patient's doctor. No answer.

While Carolyn and Dr. Smith discussed the dosage of a beta-blocker to give to bring down the man's blood pressure, Devon explained to Mr. Waters that his heart had gone into a rhythm that would require ongoing medication and monitoring. "We're going to start you on some medication now, but you're going to need to go to the hospital so that they can monitor you more closely. Do you have a preference which one?"

"The hospital? Can't you just give me the medication and let me go home? This surgery is going to be enough of a bother—I don't need this. I've had to hire help for the bakery, but I'm planning on returning next week. I'll be limited in what I can do, but I can at least help with the customers. If I go to the hospital, some doctor is going to want me to take more time off."

"I know your wife is in the waiting room. Is it okay if I talk to her and explain what is happening?" Devon asked. It wasn't going to do the man's blood pressure any good to get him more upset.

"Of course you can tell her—she's my wife." Mr. Waters stopped talking as Michael walked up beside her. "Michael, do you know they're trying to send me to the hospital?"

"I do. And I agree. Atrial fibrillation isn't something to play around with, Jim. Let me explain a little about it." As Michael explained the heart arrhythmia to Mr. Waters, Devon tried to call Dr. Morgan again. When he didn't answer, she walked out and found Mrs. Waters sitting anxiously in the waiting room. After explaining exactly what was happening with her husband and the need for him to be transferred to a local hospital, Devon returned to the recovery room.

"I still can't get Dr. Morgan on the phone, but I don't think we should wait much longer. I know it's unusual to transfer a patient without the patient's surgeon speaking with the emergency room doctor, but I don't think we have a choice," she told Michael. "I don't know Dr. Morgan, but I don't think there are many doctors who would take the news that their patient was transferred to a hospital without their knowledge very well."

"And I don't know a lot of doctors who ignore nurses' calls the way he's done today. As of now, Mr. Waters has agreed to me taking over his care and I'll be handling the transfer. If Dr. Morgan has a problem with that, he'll have to take it up with me."

As Michael pulled out his phone and made the call, Devon smiled. Over the years she had seen several doctors ignore nurses' concerns, even at the risk of their patients' well-being. She'd even seen administration side with a doctor when everyone, including them, knew the doctor was out of line. It was good to know that Michael wasn't like that. And she was pretty sure this wasn't going to end very well for Dr. Morgan.

But when she looked back at Mr. Waters, she noticed the way his hands clutched the bed railings. Looking up at the monitors, she saw that the man's heart rate was continuing to climb. She knew what had to be done, but she wasn't the one to make that call. She looked around and saw that the anesthesiologist had left the recovery room. "Dr. Hart, I need you over here."

While she waited for Michael to finish his call, she pulled the resuscitation cart up beside the bed and started opening drawers. She found the pads she knew they would need, then began to attach them to Mr. Waters.

"More of these sticky things?" the man asked, his temper starting to become short, not that she could blame him. "That nice nurse I had gave me something for the pain, but it doesn't seem to be helping much."

"The medication isn't working. He needs to be cardioverted," Devon said the moment Michael joined her. "Trust me, I've seen this before."

"You're right. I'm not a cardiologist, but I did see this before in residency. I want to have the anesthesiologist here in case we need him," Michael said, then turned to Carolyn, who'd returned. "Call Dr. Smith. Get him back in here, now. Then draw up five of morphine."

As Carolyn made the call, Mr. Waters moaned and she looked up to see that his heart rate was now in the 180s.

"Is everything ready?" Michael asked Devon. "As soon as Dr. Smith is here, I want to get this done. At these rates, his risk of going into ventricular fibrillation and cardiac arrest is just too high to wait."

"The pads are applied and I've got the machine ready. It's monophasic so I was going to set it to two hundred joules. Is that what you want?" It was funny how all that studying she'd done for her advanced cardiac life support certificate was returning now.

"We'll start at two hundred and hope that does it. If not, we'll go up to three-sixty the next time," Michael said.

The doors opened and Dr. Smith came in. Michael explained what they were about to do to Mr. Waters while the anesthesiologist listened and agreed with the plan.

"I'm not going to lie to you, Jim. It's going to

be uncomfortable, but Carolyn is going to give you some morphine to help." Michael nodded to Carolyn and she began to push the medicine through their patient's IV. As soon as the medicine was in, he looked over at Devon. "We're set at two hundred joules?"

Devon nodded and hit the charging button. "Charging now. Everyone clear."

As soon as the machine told her it was charged, she looked at Michael, then hit the button. She watched as poor Mr. Waters yelled out and his body came off the bed as the shock went through him.

They all looked up at the monitor, each of them holding their breath as the heart rate recorded a spike before it returned, this time at a rate where they could see by the individual *P* waves that the cardioversion had worked.

"Good job, everyone," Michael said, before turning to her. "Well done."

The doors opened to the recovery entrance and the ambulance crew came in with their stretcher. As Carolyn gave a report to the EMTs, Devon put her shaking hands into her pockets and stepped away.

"That was a good call," Michael said, praising her.

"Thank you for trusting me," she said, surprised by how much that really meant to her.

"Of course I trust you," Michael said, then joined Carolyn with the EMTs.

For a moment, his words made her feel amazing. Then she thought about the secret she'd been keeping from him and wondered if he would ever trust her again after she told him the truth about Conner.

CHAPTER FIVE

DEVON WASN'T SURE when she'd become one of *those* parents. The kind who get so involved in their kids' sports that they concentrate on each play as if it was somehow going to make a difference to their child getting into a good college or gaining a professional sports contract. Maybe it was because Conner had been so wound up on the way to the football field. Or maybe it was because she knew her son would be disappointed if their team lost this game. Or maybe it was just the competitive football spirit she'd grown up around. No matter what the reason, when her son walked onto the field, she found herself holding her breath and crossing her fingers.

She watched as the center snapped the ball. Everyone in the bleachers seemed to let out a breath when, instead of the quarterback dropping the ball, as he had the last two times, he held on to it then handed it off to Conner. Devon's hand went to her chest, her heart pounding hard against her ribs. This was the play that her son had told her about. The one he'd sworn Coach Hart had picked out especially for him because he was the fastest runner. As Conner broke through the other team's defensive line, Devon knew that her son was running as fast as his little legs could take him. Then Devon saw that there was a boy from the other team playing safety, waiting to tackle her son.

"Turn, Conner, turn," she yelled as she jumped up out of her seat, sending her water bottle flying down between the bleachers to the ground. She watched as her son made the necessary adjustment to his path and then turned on the speed. The woman next to her grabbed ahold of Devon's sleeve as they watched Conner pass the ten-yard line, then enter the end zone. The sidelines burst into screams and applause as Devon and the woman next to her hugged her and laughed.

"His daddy has to be so proud," the woman said before turning to the person on the other side of her.

Devon's eyes instantly went to Michael as he ran up to Conner and slapped him on the back, almost knocking her son down. Then the two of them both looked up to where she stood in the stands, their faces wide with smiles so identical that she found herself frozen in place. Could anyone else see the resemblance? How could Michael not see it when he looked down at Conner smiling like he was right then? Didn't he see the way Conner's smile was just a little crooked, exactly like his own? Didn't he recognize those startling, light green eyes?

How much longer would she be able to keep Conner's parentage a secret when to her eyes it seemed so obvious?

She spent the rest of the game in stunned silence as the other parents and visitors screamed and cheered the home team on to victory. If Conner ran another play, she couldn't recall. All she knew, as she left the stands and headed down to where the parents met their kids, was that she had to tell Michael about Conner. She'd waited, with the excuse of wanting to make sure Michael was someone she wanted in Conner's life, but she was beginning to see that it had simply been an excuse to put off telling him. She dreaded the look in his eyes when he finally knew the truth. She was so afraid that he wouldn't understand the reason for the choice she'd made, but the longer she waited, it seemed to be more of a deception than she'd ever thought it to be.

And what about after she told him? Zach had believed that Michael would understand and that the two of them would be able to make things work, as long as they put Conner first, something she'd always thought she had done. But what about Michael? She'd watched him with the kids he coached, especially Conner, and could see that he really seemed to care about them. But could she trust him to understand that what was best for Conner was to keep his life as normal as possible? Or would he be so angry that he would fight her for custody of her son?

As she headed onto the field, she saw Michael kneeling down on the ground in front of Conner as he helped her son get his shoulder pads off, while the little boy's mouth seemed to be running ninety to nothing.

"Mom, did you see me? Did you see me make that touchdown?" Conner said as he rushed up and hugged her. Unable to help herself, she pulled him closer to her. He was hot and sweaty, but she didn't care. She held on to him as if at any moment someone might pry him out of her arms. "Mom, you're squeezing too tight."

"I think you've left your mom speechless, something I've never seen before," Michael teased as he walked up to them.

"Really?" Conner asked him as he pulled away from her. "She says I'm a jabber box because I ask questions all the time. Is she a jabber box, too?"

"Maybe not now, but she definitely was one when she was your age. I remember hearing her grandma call her that exact same thing when we were growing up. I'm afraid you've inherited it from her, so it's really all her fault," Michael said with a wink.

"You hear that, Mom? It's not my fault. Next time Ms. Jordan gets on to me for talking to Max in class, I'm going to tell her it's not really my fault."

"If I get another note from Ms. Jordan about you talking in class when you're not supposed to, you're going to lose your game system for a week, no matter whose fault you think it is." Devon's instinct was telling her to grab Conner and run to the car before it was too late.

"I was talking to Conner before the game and he asked if he could see my Claymont Trophy. I told him I'd be home all weekend if you'd like to bring him by."

"Can we go, Mom?" Conner asked, his eyes pleading with her.

"Have you already forgotten about the sleepover? You're going to Max's tomorrow night and you're going to be there most of Saturday,"

Devon said, glad that she didn't have to make an excuse for turning down Michael's invitation.

"But I'll be home Saturday night, right? We could go then or Sunday," Conner persisted as his hands came up and wrapped around her waist again. "Pretty please, Mom."

"Let's wait and see how tired you are Saturday night, hey? Max's dad has a lot planned for the two of you," Devon said. Then, knowing her son was not going to let this invitation go easily, she changed the subject. "How about we stop by the Burger Barn and grab a couple burgers on the way home?"

"Can Coach Hart come, too?" Conner asked, then turned to Michael before she could stop him. "Don't you want to go, Coach Hart?"

When Michael looked at her, as if to ask permission, there was no way she could not invite him without looking rude. "Would you like to join us? Unless you have other plans, that is."

She half expected him to say that he had to get back to his office to work. She'd heard through Shalonda that she was consulting with some recruiters to hire someone to take on an administrator role at the surgical center, but he was still handling everything until someone was hired.

"That sounds good. Let me help pack up our gear and I'll meet you there," Michael said, though he looked at her as if he knew she had been hoping he'd turn down her invitation.

Twenty minutes later, Devon found herself sitting across the booth from Michael and Conner. For once she was glad of her son's ability to talk nonstop as he asked Michael question after question about his football career. There was a moment of peace when their burgers arrived and all three of them bit into the juicy sandwiches the place was known for. Looking up, she saw that Michael was staring at her.

"Hold on," he said, before reaching over and wiping her mouth with his napkin. Their eyes met and something sparked between the two of them. Devon's face went hot and she looked away too quickly, causing her head to spin for a moment.

She didn't have to ask herself what had just happened. It was more than a déjà vu moment for her as she was suddenly back in high school, sitting beside a bonfire on the beach with her friends. She'd tried to ignore Michael when he'd sat down beside her. She knew that he only thought of her as one of his brother's friends. She wasn't pretty like Lisa, the cheerleader he'd just broken up with earlier that year. She was his housekeeper's daughter. Someone he'd known all his life. Self-conscious and unsure of what to do, she'd popped one of the marshmallows she'd just roasted into her mouth. She'd jumped when Michael's finger had come up and wiped some of the gooey candy off her lips. Then she'd made the biggest mistake of her young life. She'd looked up into those green eyes of his and had been totally mesmerized. She'd closed her own eyes, thinking that he was going to kiss her then. But when she'd opened them again, Michael had moved away from her. For a moment, she'd thought maybe she'd imagined it, that heated look she'd seen in his eyes. But she knew she hadn't. Just like she knew she hadn't imagined what had just passed between the two of them now. Unable to help herself, she looked back at Michael and saw the recognition in his face. He'd felt it, too.

For the rest of the meal, she kept her eyes on Conner as he continued to pepper Michael with his continuous questions, afraid of what she might see in Michael's eyes if she looked over at him. The two of them already had a complicated relationship just because he was her boss and they'd also once been lovers. Add in the fact that Michael would soon find out that he was Conner's father, and what revealing that secret would do for their relationship, and the last thing they needed was to complicate it more. So no matter how much those little butterflies were fluttering in her stomach whenever he looked at her, she had to ignore them. If not for herself, at least for her son.

CHAPTER SIX

MICHAEL SAT ON his balcony drinking his morning coffee, wondering what it would be like to not have to start his Saturday with a trip to his office. He could count on one hand the number of days he hadn't had to spend at his office since he'd opened the surgical center. What would he do with his time when he turned over all the tedious admin work that was constantly piling up on his desk? He knew he didn't really need to be the person that approved the budget increase for the center's environmental services. Devon had been right. He wasn't able to keep juggling all the things that it took to keep the place running. The surgical center was growing faster than he'd ever imagined. Next month would be the grand opening of their new physical therapy center, which meant even more work. It was all too much for one person and there were still five months until Matt finished his residency and joined him. He didn't want to admit it, but it had partly been his ego that had made him want to hang on to all those day-to-day operations that he was now drowning in. He had taken on the task of running the Hart Sports Institute and admitting that he couldn't do it was the same as admitting failure, something he was not good at.

When his football career had come to an end, he'd been at such a loss over what to do next. He'd made the mistake of building his whole life around his success as a quarterback that he hadn't done much else. He'd lived the game, avoiding anything that could pull his attention away from his goal of making it as a professional athlete. And when he'd finally made it there? He'd worked even harder to stay.

He'd ignored everything else in his life, if it could have been called a life. He'd been so self-centered that he'd let most of his friendships go over the years, as he became more and more dedicated to succeeding. He'd even neglected his brother when he'd needed him the most. The only people he'd spent time with had been just like him—driven to succeed in a career that could end at any moment. And then, that moment had come and he'd had nothing left to work for.

He sat his cup on the side table with a little more force than was necessary, sloshing the dark brown liquid onto the table. How had he not seen that he was doing the same thing again? He'd been back in his hometown for over a year now, and aside from helping out with the kids' football team and an occasional get-together with his high school friends, all he'd done was work.

He stood and looked out over the gulf waters and saw a lone surfer about to catch a wave as the high tide sent waves crashing against the shore. While a lot of his friends and his younger brother had grown up surfing, he'd only tried it a few times. He'd preferred fishing to surfing, something that he had shared with his father. But when was the last time he'd had a fishing reel in his hand? Maybe that was something he could look forward to doing when the new administrator was hired.

He looked down the beach and saw a woman walking, her head down as she studied the packed sand just outside of the waves. She was probably searching for shells that had come ashore during the night. When she stopped and kneeled down, he knew he had been right. Then she stood and held something up to the sky, her face turned up. The sunlight highlighted the copper tint to the blond waves that draped over her shoulders. He watched as the wind picked up Devon's gorgeous hair and blew it all around her, as she held her arms out and twirled around with the happiness of a child finding a great treasure.

He laughed, and before he realized what he was doing, he took the stairs down from his balcony, stepped onto the beach, and began walking toward her. He could take a few moments before he headed to the office. He was mesmerized by the happy expression he could see on her face. It was as if she had cast some spell on him, drawing her to him.

It was the same type of feeling he'd had the night they'd run into each other in the hotel. There had been something magical about the way he'd been drawn so strongly to her. From the moment he'd recognized her, those copper highlights flashing in the light from the chandelier hanging above her, he'd been held captive by the sight of her. They'd both been so surprised at seeing each other, they'd found a booth at the hotel bar to catch up. She'd explained that she was there to meet some girlfriends for a night out, but she was early and had a few minutes to spare. When those minutes had led to an hour, she'd texted her friends that she was held up. Then he'd canceled his plans to meet up with a teammate and had invited her to supper. He couldn't have been more surprised when supper and a simple good-night kiss had led to them spending the night together. Thinking about that night again made him wonder what kissing Devon now would be like. Would he still experience that wild desire he'd felt back then?

When she turned and began to walk the other way, he found himself jogging toward her.

"Sunshine, wait," he called out to her, then slowed when she turned back toward him.

"Hey there. Isn't it a beautiful morning?" she said as he caught up with her.

The smile on her face seemed to light him up inside. For a moment, he just stood there, unable to take his eyes off her. "Yes. The most beautiful."

When her face reddened, he had no doubt she knew he was talking about her, but he didn't want to make her feel uncomfortable. "Gathering shells this morning?"

She looked down at the perfectly intact pink scallop shell she held in her hands. "Just the one. It's all I need. I'll leave the rest of them for the serious collectors."

"I take it Conner is still at his sleepover," he said, knowing she'd never leave her son alone at home.

"He is, and the house was way too quiet last night without him. I sometimes give him a hard time about the way he's constantly talking and always asking questions, but I actually love the fact that he always wants to share his thoughts and questions with me."

"He's a great kid. I'm no expert, but I think he's always asking those questions because he's so smart," Michael said as he walked with her toward her home.

"I've seen you with the children on the team. You're great with them," she said. "It makes me wonder why you haven't started a family of your own. Don't you want kids?"

"I'd love to have kids. I envy what you have with Conner. I'd be happy with one just like him."

A wave came roaring toward them and he made a grab for her arm to steady her as it rolled back out, taking the sand from under their feet with it. Her hand clutched his and she held on to him until they had made it to higher ground.

"Sorry about that," she said as if embarrassed that she'd reached out for him.

"Don't be. I'd never let you fall, Sunshine." His free hand came up to move the strands of hair that had fallen around her face.

His arm came out and steadied her as she stumbled, and her sandal fell off. "Be careful. You wouldn't believe how many injuries I've seen from wearing those shoes on the beach."

"I'm fine," she said, though her voice was unsteady.

"Are you hurt? Did you turn your ankle?" he asked, bending down to check out the shoeless foot.

"No, I said I'm fine," Devon insisted, her voice still shaking as she pulled her hand from his and picked up her shoe. "It's just what you said. About envying me for having Conner."

She stood there in front of him looking at him as if he'd just slapped her. "Because Conner's your child, Michael. He's your son."

Michael tried to comprehend what she was saying. Conner, his child? How was that possible? He'd always assumed that she was married when she had her son. Their son?

"I don't understand. How is that possible?" he asked, though he was starting to put things together. He always marked his calendar on the day he'd been injured on the football field. This year had made it eight years. Conner played on the football team of seven-year-olds, so…

A shout came from the water and they both stood and stared at where an older teenage boy, the one Michael had seen earlier riding the waves, was struggling to drag something large and dark from the water up to the beach.

"What is that?" Devon asked as they headed toward the boy.

"I'm not sure, but…" Then he realized what they were seeing. The teenager was dragging someone dressed in a diving suit out of the water.

Devon must have realized what it was, too, because they both began running at the same time, splashing out into the waves. When they reached them, Michael took the man from him and Devon helped the boy onto the shore.

"I found him out there. He was trying to make it to the beach but then he just stopped," the teen said. "And then I saw the blood. He had a spear in his hand when I first saw him. He must have cut himself with it. He dropped it on the way in."

Michael laid the man on the ground just above the waves and began assessing the situation. He put his fingers to the man's neck and felt a pulse. Then the man took in a deep breath and coughed, a little water running out of his mouth. He needed to turn him onto his side to help with that, but he also needed to find where all the blood that was running down his suit was coming from.

"I'm calling nine-one-one," Devon said from beside him as she pulled her phone from her wet shorts. Michael could only hope it wasn't damaged as he'd been in too much of a hurry to get to Devon earlier to grab his own phone.

"Sir, can you hear me?" Michael asked as he raised the man's eyelids and saw they were equal. Michael's mind was whirling from everything Devon had just told him, but he had to block it out. Right now, he had to think like a doctor, not like a man who'd just had his world turned upside down with the news that he had a seven-year-old son.

He started down the man's wet suit looking for an injury. When he got to one of the man's knees, he saw a tear in the black suit and a stream of blood flowing out. He pulled off his shirt and held it tightly against the injury. The man groaned and pulled away from where Michael was putting pressure on, and he considered that a good sign. There was no way to know how much blood he'd lost, or how much water he'd swallowed, but his response to pain was encouraging. With Michael's other hand, he continued down the man's body, as he worked through the triage process. Though he didn't see any other injuries, he couldn't be sure until the suit was removed.

"We've got a problem," Devon said, joining him beside the man. "There's a pileup on the interstate that's blocking State Road Eighty-seven.

Everyone in the county is at the accident. Dispatch says they'll send someone from the north end of the county but they couldn't give me an ETA. I told them I was a nurse and had a doctor with me and that I would call back as soon as I knew the extent of the patient's injuries."

This was the last news Michael wanted to hear, but he made himself remain calm. If they could stop the bleeding, maybe they'd be able to keep the man stable until the EMTs arrived. "The blood is coming from his knee. I think it's some kind of bite. Maybe shark or barracuda, as it sounds like he was spear fishing. We need to get him out of this suit, so I can make sure he's not bleeding anywhere else. If you'll keep the pressure here, I'll unzip the suit."

"Is he going to be alright?" the teen asked. Michael looked over and saw that he couldn't be much more than eighteen and was shaking uncontrollably.

"I don't know, but I can tell you that he wouldn't have had a chance if you hadn't gotten him out of the water," Michael said, praising the teen.

"You did good, Kyle. I can't wait to tell your mom. She's going to be so proud of you," Devon added, apparently recognizing him.

As Devon kept the pressure on, Michael

worked the man's arms, and then his legs, carefully out of the wet suit. Not finding any other injury, he went back to his right knee. "It looks like a bite. A big fish bite. Maybe a bull shark or a barracuda. I can see penetration holes to the front of the knee and it looks like there's also damage to some of the tendons, and maybe the ligaments on the side and back. Those probably happened when he was trying to get free. His pupils are equal and he responds to pain, so that's good."

"The pressure is helping, but the bleeding's still not stopped," Devon reported. Michael looked down and saw that his shirt was saturated with bright red blood.

"Yeah, I'm afraid there's a bleeder in there that needs to be tied off, but I can't do anything about it right now. If I was at the office, I'd have the equipment I needed. But here? On the beach? The best I have is a first-aid kit." Although now that he was thinking about it, there was a hemostat and a couple sutures in there that he had added. There also was a bottle of saline to be used for cleaning wounds, too.

"What about a tourniquet?" Devon asked.

"We don't have anything that would apply the kind of pressure we need." While Michael had never had the experience of doing something like this out in the field, he'd handled enough traumas during his residency that he knew what he was thinking about could be done.

"Kyle, do you see that house over there? The blue one with the big two-story balconies?" Michael asked.

"Yeah, why?" Kyle asked. "Is there someone there that can help?"

"No, it's my house. I need you to run to the house and look in the bathroom on the bottom floor. It's on the other side of the kitchen. Open the cabinets and you'll see a big first-aid kit. It looks like a small, zippered suitcase. Grab that and a couple of towels, and bring it out here to me."

Kyle hesitated for just a moment, then he looked at the man lying on the sand, turned, and sprinted up the beach to Michael's home.

The silence between the two of them after Kyle left was stifling as they waited. Finally, he couldn't take it any longer. "Why didn't you tell me?"

"It's too complicated to discuss right now," Devon said, her hands beginning to shake from where she was holding pressure.

"Let's switch places and you can do a pulse check," Michael said. He knew she was right, yet even as he worked to keep this patient alive

Devon's words—*he's your son*—kept replaying over and over in his mind.

"His pulse is in the one-tens," Devon said. "His respirations are high at twenty-four."

"The high pulse is probably because of the blood loss," he said. "The respirations are probably because of the water in his lungs."

The moment that Kyle returned carrying the supplies, Michael lifted the bloody shirt. He could see that most of the bleeding from the tearing wound had stopped. It was at the puncture site where he could see there was still blood pooling in the tissue.

Devon kneeled down beside him and laid out one of the towels as calmly as if it was a surgery towel and she was setting up for surgery. She put on a pair of gloves, then offered him a pair. She laid out several packages of gauze, opened one, and handed it to him.

"Can you call nine-one-one and see if they can give you an ETA?" Michael said as he put on the gloves. If he knew there was help on the way, he'd just pack the wound and wait for the first responders to transfer the man to the hospital.

While Devon made the call, he took the gauze and cleared out the blood so he could get a better view of the damage. Like he had thought, it looked like there was only one vessel that was continuing to bleed. If the man hadn't already lost so much blood on the way out of the water, he wouldn't be worried about it.

"Dispatch says they're still fifteen minutes out. I'm going to stay on the phone so I can let them know when I see them," Devon said.

"I can run up to the road and flag them down," Kyle said, then jumped up and ran down to the beach entrance.

Calculating the time it would take to transfer the man to the hospital, especially if they couldn't use the interstate, Michael made the only decision he could. "I can see the vessel that's bleeding. If you can keep the blood out of my way, I'm going to clamp it. We can leave the clamp on until we get him to the hospital, then I can take him to the operating room and clean the wound out and tie off anything that's left bleeding then."

Devon looked at him and, to his surprise, she smiled. "Let's do it."

With the bleeding vessel right at the entrance of the bite mark, Michael used the tip of the clamp to maneuver it as Devon cleared the blood out of the way. With one click, the hemostat stopped the blood flow and Michael relaxed.

They had just finished applying a large gauze bandage to the site when they heard the sirens.

As the first responders made their way down the beach toward them, Michael recognized one of the EMTs.

"It looks like a bite. A big fish bite. Maybe a bull shark or it could be a barracuda. There's a penetration wound to his right knee with some damage to the tendons and ligaments."

"His pupils are equal and he does respond to pain, but he hasn't been conscious. His pulse is in the one-tens and his respirations are fast," Devon added.

"We think he might have been spear fishing when it happened. Kyle saw the man trying to get to shore and then saw him go still. He dragged him in and called for help. I suspect he's got some water in his lungs, though," Michael said.

The EMT looked over at Michael as he dropped down beside them. "Oh, hey, Doc. I didn't recognize you there without your shirt on."

Then the man turned to where Kyle sat with Devon's arm around him. "Way to go, Kyle."

Kyle, still pale, nodded at him.

"This is Doctor Hart. He opened that new sports surgical center. He did my dad's knee surgery last month," the EMT said casually, as another man joined them and began to hook up all the monitors and prepare their patient for transport.

When they offered for Michael to ride along with them, he turned back to Devon, but she waved him off. “Go ahead. I’m going to give Kyle a ride home.”

After climbing in beside the EMT, Michael looked back to where Devon stood, one of her arms still draped around the teen’s shoulder as she spoke with him. Then she looked up and her eyes went to Michael. There was so much for the two of them to discuss. He wanted to know the reason for her keeping his son’s existence from him. He had thought he knew her. But the girl he’d always called Sunshine would do never something like this.

None of this made sense. All he knew was that once this patient had been stabilized, he was going to get some answers.

CHAPTER SEVEN

As soon as Devon had gotten Conner settled in bed for the night, she had curled up in her grandmother's chair with a soft knitted blanket draped over her legs as she watched the street traffic for any sign of Michael returning from the hospital. He'd called her hours ago to tell her that the man, a chief from the local air force base, had been identified, and that he was in stable condition after receiving a couple liters of blood and plasma. He'd agreed to accept the patient and was about take him into surgery to clean out his wound and hopefully repair some of the damage.

He'd asked her about Kyle. The boy had been visibly shaken up by what he'd seen, but Devon had reassured him that he'd been okay once she'd got him to his parents. She'd told him that seeing that six-foot eighteen-year-old falling into his five-foot-nothing mom's arms, and bursting into tears, had brought tears to her own eyes.

Then he'd told her he wasn't expecting the surgery to take too long and he would like to stop by to see her on his way home. She'd wanted to put him off, but she knew she couldn't. It was time to tell Michael the whole truth about Conner.

The moment Michael had admitted how much he'd envied her for having a son like Conner, she'd known she couldn't keep his son from him any longer. Through all the years while she'd wondered about Michael and even those occasional times when she had doubts about keeping Conner from him, she'd never thought that he could be out there wishing that he had a child. His confession had hit her hard. Too hard for her to ignore it. How could she?

She'd always been able to tell herself that Michael was living the life he'd wanted. Even when he'd announced to the sports networks that he wouldn't be returning to the field, but instead would be putting all of his energy into going back to college to become the best orthopedic surgeon he could be, she'd thought she was doing the right thing. He'd devoted his life from that moment on to helping athletes, instead of being one. And from what she could see, he'd more than exceeded his dream.

Now, knowing that he'd actually envied her life with her son—their son—all along, the guilt she felt over a decision she'd made eight years ago was suffocating.

She sat up straight, her hands tightening on the blanket as a truck she didn't recognize pulled into her driveway. The passenger door opened and she saw Michael as he climbed out and waved at the driver.

She stood as he walked onto the porch to join her. His steps were slow and his normally bright eyes had dimmed. "Did everything go okay?"

He sat down hard, not waiting for her to sit. "He'll make it, but there was a lot of damage to that knee. I did the best I could, but there was extensive muscle damage. The good news is I was able to clean out the damaged tissue and it should heal well. But he'll need some time in rehabilitation and I don't know if this will affect his career as a pilot."

"I'm sure you did everything that you could," she said, but Devon could see that Michael wasn't satisfied with what he'd been able to do. "You of all people know that things happen sometimes that send us on a different path from the one we were expecting to take. His path might change, or maybe this will just be a temporary side trip."

"You're right. All of our paths change through life. My own life might not be what I had envisioned when I was younger, but now…" He paused for a moment, then ran his hands through his hair, pushing it back off his face. "After what I was able to be a part of in the OR today, knowing that I helped that man today, I honestly wouldn't change a thing."

"But we do all have things we would do differently, right? Sometimes we find ourselves at forks in the road where we have to make decisions we're not prepared for and we do the best we can." Devon certainly knew she'd been in that position several times in her life. Not just when she'd made the decision not to keep trying to tell Michael about the pregnancy when she couldn't initially get through to him, but also when she'd decided to marry Zach, knowing that they weren't in love with each other. Then there had been Zach's death and the promise she'd made to him to tell Michael about his son. She just hoped she could make Michael understand why she'd made the decision that she'd made about her son. Their son.

"Tell me, Devon. What in the world could have caused you to keep from telling me that I had a son?" Though Michael hadn't raised his voice, his words left her in no doubt of his anger.

"I don't blame you for being angry. I didn't

set out to hurt you, though I can see now that I have."

"Hurt me? You just turned my life upside down. I just want to know how this happened. And what about your husband? Did he know? Were the two of you already together the night we ran into each other at the hotel?"

His words stung, but she couldn't blame him for what he was thinking when he hadn't been given any explanation.

"Yes, Zach knew. Zach… He was a good man. And, no, we weren't together, not as a couple. I met Zach during my freshman year of college. He was a computer science major and had IT geek written all over him. He was in my English composition class and when he saw me struggling with formatting for our first assignment, he offered to help. From there we became friends. The two of us and a couple other nursing students rented a house off campus our senior year." She paused, then laughed. "He said he regretted letting me talk him into moving in with us the first time he opened the refrigerator and found a dissected frog on a plate beside the ketchup."

He stood and moved away from her, and for some reason she followed him. "We were just friends then. Good friends, but no more. Then I found out that I was pregnant."

"And you told him and not me?" he said. He turned toward her and the pain she saw in his eyes cut through her chest.

Her hands grabbed ahold of his arms and she forced herself to look him in the eye. "You never called me after our night together. But after you were injured, I called several times to check on you. Even before I knew I was pregnant I called. I wanted to hear your voice. I wanted to make sure you were okay. But Matt said you weren't taking any calls. I knew if that night we had shared had meant anything to you, you would have called me back, but still I called."

He made a small sound of distress.

"I wasn't angry. That wasn't what this was about." Yes, she'd felt hurt, but no matter how angry he might be at her about what she had done, she didn't want him to think that it had been meant as some type of revenge. "Three weeks later, when I knew I was pregnant, I called you again. Matt said that you were in a bad way. He said that it looked like your career was over and you weren't taking the news very well, and that you weren't taking any calls. When I asked him if he had told you that I'd called, he said he had. Then I asked him to please have you call me back, as it was important."

When his eyes turned away from her, she let go of him. Even after all this time, and knowing how his football injuries had affected him, the way he'd forgotten about her after that night still hurt. "I never meant for that night in the hotel to happen. But I was young and thought that what happened between us, the kind of passion I had experienced that night with you, meant something special."

His shoulders stiffened.

"When you didn't ever call me back, I knew that it hadn't meant the same thing to you. So when I found out I was pregnant and alone, I did what I thought was best for me and my child. Zach had cancer as a child and the radiation treatment he received meant he wasn't able to father children, so he offered to marry me. My grandmother was already very sick. Her finding out that I had followed in my mother's footsteps and was pregnant without a father for my baby would have killed her. The stress would have been too much."

For a moment, neither of them said anything, the roar of the waves across the street the only sound in the dark night.

"So why tell me now?" Michael asked, turning to her, his face a cold mask that she had never seen before. She was surprised to find how much more that hurt. But what had she expected? For him to suddenly apologize for not calling her all those years ago? Or for him to suddenly declare his undying love for her? When would she finally accept that she had never meant anything more to him than just being a friend with benefits?

"Because of Zach. Before he died, he made me promise to tell you." Unable to stand any longer, she sat back down in her grandmother's rocking chair.

"You should have found some way to tell me," Michael said, his voice even and his words clipped.

She ignored his words. Whether she had been right or wrong, she had made the only decision she believed she could make at the time. She looked up at the stars and prayed for Conner's sake that she had made the right decision both back then in marrying Zach, and in telling Michael now. The gulf breeze had died down and the air was heavy with humidity. The neighborhood was so quiet tonight that she felt completely alone, even though Michael stood in front of her. Her heart grew heavier with each moment that he remained silent.

Then, without saying a word, he started back down the porch steps. She stood and watched him walk away.

"Goodbye, Mickey," she whispered, as he disappeared into the darkness of the night.

CHAPTER EIGHT

THE MOMENT HE'D gotten home, he'd changed into his running gear and taken off down the beach. While his form wasn't what it had been before his injuries, he'd managed to build up his speed over the years, yet his mind still raced faster than his legs could go. Before he knew it, he was over a mile from his home.

He turned to run back, but found that he'd spent all his angry frustration and now felt empty and without the energy he needed to return. So he sat down, right there on the damp sand, and tried to make sense of everything he'd learned that night.

He'd tried his best to listen to everything Devon had said, but after her announcement that he was Conner's father, the rest had been so hard to hear. He attempted to dissect it all now, looking for something that would explain how it was possible that he had a son he'd never known about, but he couldn't seem to put it all together.

But there was one thing that had struck him when Devon had been talking that she had only hinted at. Everything that had happened from the moment she'd left that hotel room would have been different if he'd only called her and told her how much that night had meant to him. What would have happened after that, he wasn't sure. He'd been so tied up in his career and she was still in college. But he did know with certainty that if he'd made that call he wouldn't have missed the last seven years of his son's life. If he'd given Devon any hint that he wanted to continue the relationship, things would have been completely different.

Thinking of that call that had never happened, he pulled his phone from his pocket. He saw that it was after eleven and knew that his brother was probably asleep, but this couldn't wait until the morning.

"Hello," Matt said, his voice too alert for him to have been sleeping. There was the sound of a radio like those used by emergency services in the background.

"Hey, it sounds like you're at the hospital. Do you have a minute?" Michael asked. He shouldn't have called. Not until he'd had more time to think things through. To find some way to comprehend what finding out about Conner would mean to his life.

"Hold on," Matt said. There was the sound of movement and then a door shutting. "Sorry about that. They just brought in this kid riding a motorcycle that had been hit by a car. He has an open femur fracture, but they're taking him to CT first, to make sure there aren't any other injuries before I can take him to surgery."

"It sounds like you have a lot going on. I can call you tomorrow." If his brother was going into the OR shortly, Michael didn't want to say anything that might cause him to not be able to concentrate.

"Mickey, it's late. We both know you wouldn't have called if there wasn't something on your mind. What's going on?"

Michael knew now wasn't the time to discuss this, but he couldn't hold this back any longer. "You know I told you that Devon had come home. Did I tell you that she had a son?"

"I don't think so. Why?"

"Because it ends up that her seven-year-old son, Conner, is mine." As Michael said the words, he felt something settle in his chest. He'd been so shocked by everything Devon had told him that he hadn't been concentrating on the most important part. Conner, the boy he'd laughed with, and played with, and already come to care about—that child was his son.

"Okay, hold on. Didn't you tell me that Devon had been married? That her husband had died?"

"He had cancer. Apparently he'd had cancer as a child and it returned. It's all very complicated."

"I guess it is complicated since I don't even understand how this is possible. I mean, you and Devon? When did this happen? And why wasn't I ever told about it?" Matthew was beginning to sound a little annoyed now.

"If you must know, it happened a couple days before I was injured. We ran into each other when I was in Tallahassee." Michael wasn't about to go into the details with his brother.

"Well, I guess that explains all her phone calls. Not that I was surprised that she called to check on you. A lot of our friends from home called. But she was definitely calling more than the rest of them. I didn't want to be rude, but she had gotten pretty insistent about speaking to you. I had to tell her straight that you didn't want to talk to anyone, which you didn't."

The line went quiet for a moment. "Oh, wow. She was trying to get in touch with you about the pregnancy, wasn't she?"

"Yes," Michael said, "it seems she was."

"Oh, man, I'm so sorry, Mickey. If I'd had any idea that there was something going on between the two of you I would have made sure you talked to her. I didn't know," Matt said, and Michael could hear the apology and the worry in his brother's voice.

"It's not your fault, Matt. It was a bad time for both of us. Or I guess for the three of us. I have regretted for years not calling Devon after that night. I was so wrapped up in that next game, and I thought I had time." He didn't have to say that time ran out on the football field shortly afterward, and it was months before he'd felt like he had any kind of life left to live. From what Devon had said, it sounded like she would have been married by then, anyway.

"So I'm an uncle?" Matt asked. "I have to say that sounds really cool. When do I get to meet this kid of yours?"

"I don't know," Michael said. "I just found out tonight. I don't know what happens next."

"What happens next is you get to know your son. That's the plan, right? I mean the two of you don't mean to keep this from him, do you? Because that would really be messed up."

Leave it to Matt to get down to what was really important. Conner, and how they were going to handle things between them, was what was really important now. It was one of the reasons it had been so helpful to have Matt beside him during all his surgeries and rehab. There hadn't been a question that his brother didn't ask, or a possible solution to a problem that he didn't research.

"Give us some time. I need to talk to Devon and figure out where the two of us go from here," Michael said.

"The two of you, huh? Is there anything else you haven't told me? Is there more going on between you again?" Matt asked, his teasing tone returning, then disappearing again. "Seriously, bro. I don't know what happened between you and Devon, but if you still care for her at all, don't let her get away again."

"Go take care of your patient. I'll call you tomorrow." With that, Michael ended the call, then stood.

He took the walk back home slowly. His mind had finally settled and he could think more clearly now. The anger he'd first felt when Devon had told him about his son had passed for now. While he still didn't agree with what she had done, he could understand a lot of her reasoning and he was willing to accept his part in her decisions. Although it was hard for him to comprehend, he was hurt that Devon hadn't known that whatever else was happening in his life, he would have taken care of her and their son. He knew she had made several efforts to get in touch with him, but couldn't she have tried just a little harder for a little longer? If she could have waited until he had recovered from the surgeries, they would have been able to talk and work things out.

And didn't he sound like the self-centered jock he'd been back then? Hadn't he learned over the years that the whole world didn't revolve around him?

The way he saw it, there were two things he could do now. He could choose to continue to be angry with Devon and her reasons for what she did. Or he could choose to put the past behind him and begin planning a future with his son. He knew what he would do in the end. He'd learned that the only way to move forward was to put the past behind him and look to the future.

He only hoped that he and Devon would be able to find a way to move forward from this together, so that he could be the father he wanted to be to his son.

The next morning, after much pleading from Conner, Devon called Michael to see if she could bring the boy over that afternoon to see his trophies. Though seeing Michael was the last thing she wanted to do, she felt this nagging need to make sure that he was okay. He'd been so upset the night before. He'd been angry, too, and she had expected that. But that he'd also seemed so hurt had surprised her.

"I told Max that I was going to see Coach Hart's trophies, and he was so jealous. I told him that maybe I could get the coach to let him come see them, too. Do you think Coach Hart would let him?" Conner asked as they crossed over the street to the beach, so they could look for any washed-up shells as they walked the couple of blocks to what had used to be Michael's parents' home.

"I think there's a good chance that he would," Devon said. For weeks her son had been calling Michael "Coach Hart" and it hadn't bothered her. Now, though, it seemed so wrong. After having Michael admit his envy over her having a son like Conner, the guilt she had felt for keeping their son a secret had multiplied exponentially.

Zach had been right. She had needed tell Michael about Conner. She only wished she had done it earlier.

"I think so, too. He's real nice like that. Maybe he could just bring them to practice one day. Then everyone could see them," Conner said before rushing off ahead of her, then stopping to examine a shell stuck in the sand. When he pulled the shell out and saw that it was broken, he threw it back into the water then ran back up to her.

"Is the only reason you and your friends like Coach Hart because he was a football star and has a bunch of trophies?" Devon asked, wanting to know if it was just hero worship that was causing her son to be so taken with Michael. Though she knew that was a part of it, she hoped Conner liked Michael for more than that. She wanted the two of them to form something deeper. Something like what Conner had had with Zach, though different. She never wanted Conner to think that Michael was replacing Zach. Keeping Zach's memory alive was important for both of them.

"I think it's cool he has all those trophies and stuff and he's a really good coach, but I don't think that's why we like him. Mostly I like him because he doesn't talk to me like I'm just a kid. And when I mess up in practice, he doesn't get mad. He just explains how I can do better next time. Some coaches on the other teams yell a lot. He doesn't yell."

She stopped at the back of Michael's home and looked up. The house had been built onto pilings to protect it from the flooding that came with living in an area frequented by hurricanes. For as long as Devon could remember, she and her grandmother had used the back entrance to the home, taking the stairs up to the balcony. It wasn't because her grandmother worked for the Harts. It was because her grandmother was considered a neighbor and a friend.

But now, looking up at the balcony stairs and knowing how things had changed between her and Michael last night, she wondered if she should have gone around to the front entrance. She was considering doing just that when Michael leaned over the railing and smiled down at the two of them. "What are you waiting for? Come on up."

Before she could stop him, Conner raced up the steps, her breath catching when he almost missed a step and had to grab ahold of the railing to keep from falling.

"Conner, slow down. There's no rush," Michael said from where he now stood at the top of the stairs. "You almost gave your mom a heart attack."

As she made it up to the last step, Michael reached out his hand to her. She stood there a moment and looked at his outstretched hand. Was this a sign he'd already forgiven her? Did he understand that she had done what she'd thought was best for their son? She looked up into his eyes. There was an uncertainty there, a vulnerability that she had never seen before. She'd hurt him more than she had thought possible and her heart cracked a little. So where did they go from here?

Making her decision, she put her hand into his with the same force that she would have used to put an operating instrument into it. There was no going back now. The two of them had to work together for Conner's sake.

He squeezed her hand and something suddenly changed between them. The uncertainty disappeared from his eyes, and was replaced by an intensity so hot that it took her breath away. Unable to look away, she stumbled on the last step up and he grabbed her. His arms came around her, pulling her to him as he steadied her. Her face warmed as a flush of heat flared through her body. She forced her eyes from his and pulled away her hand before making a show of straightening the plain white T-shirt she'd worn with her shorts that day.

"These are different," she said as moved around him to the back entrance of the house. "I remember there only being a set of French doors here."

"Those doors were worn out by the time I moved back here. One of the first things I did was have the back wall removed and replaced with these doors so I could open up the whole room when the weather is pretty. They're wind-resistant and a lot more airtight when they're closed than the old doors," Michael explained as he came up behind her.

"I love them. You must have a beautiful view of the sunsets from here," she said. She'd already been nervous about seeing Michael today after all that had been said the night before. Having this… Attraction? Desire? Well, whatever it was that had just passed between the two of them, it had to stop.

She walked into the room and tried to concentrate on the other changes that had been made to the house. He'd opened up the whole downstairs with a solid wood beam placed between the family room and what had been a galley kitchen. The beam had been stained to match the driftwood mantel over the fireplace and it gave the whole room a light, airy feel that was so different from what she remembered the last time she'd been there.

"I rarely catch one, but when I do it is spectacular," Michael said. He walked toward the kitchen and her heart began to calm with each step he took away from her. "Since I doubt you really want to look at boring trophies, how about I get you a drink and you can sit outside or inside, if you prefer?"

"Mom doesn't think trophies are boring. She put the one I got last football season up on the china case so it would be safe and we could see it every night at dinner," Conner said as he turned around in a circle in the middle of the room. Her son. She'd almost forgotten that he was even there. "Didn't your mom want you to see your trophies when you had dinner?"

"My mom and dad had someone build a big cabinet upstairs for me and my brother's trophies. Let me get your mom something to drink and we can go up," Michael said, turning back toward the kitchen again before Devon reached out a hand to stop him.

"Go ahead and take him up. I'll just get a glass of water and wait for you on the balcony." Without looking at him, she walked past him into the kitchen and, without thinking, went straight to where the glasses were kept. Even with all the changes in the house, it felt familiar to her. Michael had somehow made the home more modern while still leaving it feeling like the home where he'd grown up.

After filling her glass with water and ice from

the refrigerator, she walked outside and leaned on the railing overlooking the beach. The sky was clear except for a few puffy white clouds.

When Michael had left the night before, she'd gone over and over everything that she had said. She'd admitted to him that she had been disappointed that he hadn't called her. She'd even admitted that she had thought the night they spent together had meant something more than a one-night stand. It had been embarrassing in some ways to admit those things, but she'd wanted to be completely honest with him. Was that the reason for the way he'd looked at her? Was he remembering that night, too?

Or was this something different? There had been something happening between them for several days now. She'd tried to ignore it. She'd known that it was foolish of her to even want to explore it until things were settled between Michael and Conner. But now that her secret was out, did she feel any different?

She looked back to where she could see inside the second-floor window, where Michael and Conner stood. Her son was talking as fast as his lips could move, his eyes wide with excitement, while Michael stood beside him listening as if the kid's words were just as important as listening to one of his patients. She had to admit that though she'd had concerns about bringing a new parental figure into Conner's life, Michael seemed to be perfect for the job.

She knew in her heart that Michael was still angry with her. But she also knew that he was thrilled to learn that Conner was his son. Only time would tell if he'd ever really be able to forgive her.

She turned back to the beach and saw a couple had come to play in the waves. They looked no older than her and their laughing was so carefree that it made her smile. She remembered playing in those waves without a care in the world. She'd been much younger then. She wondered if her life would ever be like that again.

She didn't move when Michael stepped up behind her and casually put his arms on each side of the rail, then looked over her shoulder. "It looks like they're having fun down there."

"It does," she said, then turned to find herself almost in Michael's arms. Her body stiffened and her breath caught. Did he know he was doing this to her? "You didn't leave Conner alone with all those trophies, did you?"

As if he could feel the tension in her body, he stepped back and came to stand beside her. "He's safe in the game room. When I left him he was trying to figure out how to work the pinball machine. Apparently he's used to the virtual type of machine and hasn't ever seen one as 'old' as mine. He made me feel ancient."

"Get used to it. Some days just trying to keep up with him makes me feel old and decrepit." Her breath caught when she looked up at him. His smile was gone, his lips slightly parted, and his eyes were warm as he stared down into hers. "We need to talk. About Conner. But not here, where he could hear us."

The warmth in Michael's eyes disappeared. "He has to know at some point. You can't expect me to ignore the fact that he is my son."

"I know he has to be told, but we have to be careful to tell him at the right time and in the right way. He was devastated when we lost Zach. He's bound to be confused when he finds out he has another father."

"Hey, Coach Hart, do you have any more of those games? That one is a lot of fun," Conner called, as he thundered down the stairs toward them.

"Have you ever played the original *Pac-Man* game?" Michael asked as he stepped away from her.

"I don't think so," Conner said as he stepped outside with them.

She turned around and faced Michael first,

and then her son. "How about we save that for another time? Tomorrow's a school day and I need to get dinner started."

"But, Mom..." Conner began.

"If your mom says you need to go, we're not going to argue with her," Michael said. "Unless you want me to keep Conner here out of your way and when you're ready for him I can bring him home?" he added.

She started to protest, but then the two of them smiled those identical, charming, crooked smiles at her and she knew she was beat. How was it possible that no one had noticed the similarities between the two of them?

"How about I get everything ready and when Coach Hart brings you home, he can stay for dinner?" Devon watched as Michael and Conner shared high fives before heading up the stairs. The two of them, smiling and laughing, brought a bittersweet smile to her lips.

Seeing the two of them together, she now understood what Zach had tried to tell her. Her husband had known what it was like to be a father to her son. He'd loved it and he'd always let her know how grateful he was that she'd allowed him to have that experience. But he'd also felt guilty that he was taking that experience away from another man. It didn't come as a surprise to her; Zach had always been a very sensitive man. She just wished she could tell him that she understood now. That he'd been right. She couldn't help but think that somehow he knew that she had fulfilled her promise to him.

CHAPTER NINE

MICHAEL FOLLOWED DEVON out to the porch carrying each of them a glass of the wine he'd brought with him when he brought Conner home.

"I appreciate you letting Conner spend so much time with you today. He'll talk about it for days," Devon said as she took a glass from him.

The boy was certainly a handful—his mouth and feet never slowed down. He didn't know how Devon managed to keep up with him. But Michael didn't know when he'd last had as much fun as he'd had today. The hours he had spent with Conner playing those old-school arcade games had taken him right back to his own childhood. He'd been reminded of all the time he'd spent with his brother, each competing to beat the other one, in that very same game room. "I appreciate you bringing him over. He's a great kid. You and Zach did a good job raising him."

"Thank you," she said, then took a sip of the wine. "That means a lot coming from you."

"I'm sorry I left the way I did last night. All I can say is that I needed to process things."

"I don't blame you, Michael. I know hearing Conner was your son had to have been a terrible shock," Devon said, then repositioned herself in the chair.

"It was a shock. That's for sure. But it wasn't terrible. You have to know that finding out that Conner is my son..." For a moment, he found himself unable to go on. He didn't think of himself as an especially emotional man, but actually being able to say that Conner was his son touched something inside of him. Was this what being a father was like? This feeling of pride and humbleness at the same time? His father had always been quick to tell his sons how proud he was of them. He wanted to be exactly that kind of father to Conner.

He took a breath and cleared his throat. "Finding out that Conner is my son has to be the best thing that has ever happened to me. He is amazing and I couldn't be more proud of him. But I do have to ask why you didn't tell me the truth about him the first time you saw me at the center."

Devon walked to the old rocking chair and began to rock. "Conner is the reason I hesitated over taking this job. I was afraid that if I worked with you, somehow you'd find out about Conner before I was ready to tell you about him. Then, of course, I found out you were one of his football coaches."

"But why would you think me being around Conner would make a difference? There was no reason for me to question you about who his father was," he said with a puzzled look.

"Maybe it was just me, because I know the truth, but I can see so much of you in him. The way he smiles. The way he laughs. And have you ever stopped and looked at his eyes? They're the exact same light green as yours. The only other people I've ever seen with that color are Matt and your father."

"So you told me when you did because you thought I'd see the similarities between me and Conner and question if he could be mine?" Michael had always thought he was observant, but apparently he had been wrong.

"Maybe, a little. But then I saw the two of you together. You're so good with him, Michael. So patient. And then you mentioned that you would like to have had a son just like him. That you envied me having Conner. How could I not tell you then?" She leaned back in her chair and her shoulders sagged. He could see that the last twenty-four hours had to have taken as much of a toll on her as they had on him. "But I want to be honest with you. I think it is really important that we are honest with each other from now on, so I need to tell you all the truth."

Michael's mind tried to imagine what else she could have kept from him, but came up blank. "Okay, tell me."

"One of the reasons I applied for this job was because I wanted to make sure that you would be good for my son," Devon said, then looked away from him as if she was embarrassed by what she had done.

For a moment, he was taken back. "You thought I might be bad for Conner? Like I'd hurt him or something?" He thought she had hurt him before, but this cut even deeper.

"You have to understand that I didn't grow up in the same perfect world that you did. Things were different for me. Trust isn't something I give easily when it comes to my son." She turned her shoulder to him and he could see how much she wanted him to see why she'd done what she had done.

Yes, her words hurt, but she was right. He'd had an almost perfect life. Even with losing his parents, he knew the time they'd had together had been a gift. Though he'd heard all the rumors that had spread about Devon when she'd shown up at her grandmother's house, he didn't know what was real and what was fiction. How could he judge what she had done without knowing the real reason behind her actions?

"Do you want to tell me about it?" he asked gently. A part of him wanted to know how many of the rumors were true, but at the same time, he didn't want to cause her any more pain.

"Let's just say that my mother had a habit of bringing home men who weren't very nice to either of us. It seemed that no matter what I did, either one of them, or my mother, was mad at me. I think it was just because I was there. In some ways, the last man she brought around did me a favor by beating me. It was because of him that I came to live here with my grandmother."

Michael looked over at her and saw that she had quit rocking, and now, was staring out into the night. Was it possible that she was reliving that terrible experience right now?

The thought that the man who had beaten her could still hurt her like this made him angrier than he'd ever been. He walked over to Devon, and bent down in front of her. "I'm sorry that happened to you, but I am glad you came here to Silver Sands. Your grandmother loved you so much and she was so proud of you the last time I saw her."

His hands came up and brushed against her cheeks, and then up through her hair, and he found himself being unable to ignore the desire that was coming alive within his body. Hearing her talk about the abuse she'd experienced during her childhood made him ache to hold her. When he leaned toward her, his lips touched hers.

This wasn't the sweet kiss they'd shared as teenagers that night on the beach after the death of his parents. And it wasn't the desperate kisses they'd shared in a hotel room, knowing that in the morning they'd go their separate ways. He wanted this kiss to be protective and comforting. But even as he thought this, a fire seemed to come alight inside them both.

Her lips opened and his tongue swept into her mouth as he pulled her up out of the chair. Her arms came up around his neck and he felt her body relax into him. Though a part of him was afraid that she would regret this later, he had to taste her. Right now, with his lips on hers, their tongues tangling together, and her body pulled tight against him, he just didn't care about tomorrow or any of the tomorrows after that. There was only the here and now for them. He held her so tight that he could feel the beating of her heart against his chest, as his own heart seemed to try to match its rhythm. He pulled her even closer as the hard length of him pressed against her belly. He knew they had to stop before things went any further. They were standing on her front porch with the light shining over their heads. If anyone drove down the road, they'd see them.

He pulled his lips from hers reluctantly, but kept his arms around her.

"And then there was this thing… Something was happening…between us," she said as she tried to catch her breath.

"This?" Michael asked, his own breaths coming fast and shallow as he stepped away from her.

"Yes, this thing between us," she said. "It's another one of the reasons I finally told you about Conner. I couldn't let things go any further before I told you about him. I knew it would change things, but it's better for both of us this way. If I'd waited it would have made things even worse."

"And has it changed things for you?" he asked.

He couldn't deny that he had been hurt by the way Devon had kept Conner a secret from him. He would never have thought the girl he'd known as Sunshine, the sweet considerate girl who he remembered, could do something like that to him. But he also knew that she'd been young and scared at the time she'd made that decision. Last night, as he'd walked on the beach, he'd made the decision to put the past behind them and concentrate on the future he had with his son. But he hadn't been sure about what that might mean for him and Devon at the time. He'd hoped they could at least be friends again. Right now, he found himself wanting more.

"Because it hasn't changed anything for me," he said. Because, looking at the woman sitting in front of him, he knew that nothing that he'd discovered the night before had changed how he felt about her. He'd seen how she'd taken charge of emergency situations in the operating room. He'd seen how she was with his son. That was the woman she was now. That was the woman who he'd found himself drawn to over and over again since she'd returned.

"How is that possible? How can you forgive me, just like that?" she asked. "I still can't even say I regret my decision. It's too close to saying I regret my decision to marry Zach. I won't do that. Not that I don't feel guilty about what I did to you, as I do. But my life with Zach came to be because of my pregnancy."

"So where do we go from here?" he asked. He wouldn't push her. Not tonight. The truth was he was as confused about what was happening between them as she clearly was. He needed to take the time to get to know his son first, and then maybe he and Devon could explore things and see where they led. There were too many issues between them to complicate things any more than they already were.

"I don't know. I know that we'll have to tell Conner at some point. He has the right to know. Zach even said so. When we realized he wasn't going to beat the cancer this time, he told me that I needed to tell both of you the truth. He wanted Conner to have a father after he was gone."

"He must have been a remarkable man," Michael said honestly, his heart squeezing. How was he supposed to live up to a man like him?

"He was. That's why this is so hard. Maybe if Zach had been gone longer it would be easier. I don't expect you to understand this, but it seems almost disloyal to tell Conner that Zach wasn't really his father. At least not his biological father." She stepped away from him and he felt the emptiness of his arms immediately, something that he'd never felt before. "All I'm asking is that you give me a little time. Conner took Zach's death very hard. The two of them were so close. I just want to be careful and find the right way to tell him."

"I understand," he said. He knew he had to tread softly here for both Conner and Devon's sakes. "So how about this? The three of us continue to spend more time together, just like we did this weekend. That way, he'll get to know me better. Then, when we decide the time is right to tell him, he'll be more comfortable with the idea."

"We can do that," Devon said with a nod. "And thank you for understanding. I know you'll agree with me that the most important thing right now is that Conner feels loved and secure. He has to be my first priority."

Devon opened her front door, then turned back to look at him. Their eyes met, and once more he felt that fire inside him flare up. Like Devon, he couldn't describe exactly what it was that was happening between the two of them. Was it just lust they were feeling? Or was it something deeper? Either way, as he made his way across the beach to his home, he found himself looking forward to finding out not only what it was, but also just where it would take them.

When Devon arrived at work the next day, her emotions were all over the place. She wasn't sure if it was the kiss or Michael knowing about Conner that had her tied up in knots. Maybe she shouldn't have rushed into telling Michael the truth. Just bursting out with the fact that Michael was Conner's father on the beach had probably been foolish. But after listening to Michael talk about wanting a child, she couldn't have stopped herself. And if she hadn't told him then, when would she have? She'd been working with Michael for a month and hadn't been able to do it in all that time. So what? When would have been the right time? When Conner graduated from high school? Or maybe when she was lying on her deathbed?

She had to quit second-guessing herself. It was done now. The three of them had to move on from here. Michael certainly seemed to be ready to do so.

The truth was there never would have been a perfect time to tell Michael about his son. That time would have been eight years ago. And it wouldn't even have been perfect then, not with Michael trying to recover from his injuries. The last thing he had needed then was someone with whom he'd had a one-night stand showing up pregnant on his doorstep.

But what about that kiss? How were they going to be able to move on from that?

An alert message came over her work phone, the noise of it causing the patients and visitors in the waiting room to turn and stare as she walked by them. It only took a second for her to read it before she was running for the operating room. She stopped only long enough to grab a mask and hat as she passed the supply closet at the entrance to the operating suites. The front desk had been abandoned and the halls were empty.

It wasn't until she turned a corner that she saw several of the OR staff crowded outside operating room four, where the emergency had been paged out.

"Who's the doctor?" she asked as the staff parted to let her in.

"Dr. Morgan is doing an ACL repair on an eighteen-year-old male. It looks like the kid is having seizures," Robert, one of the OR techs, said.

Just hearing the doctor's name put her on alert. Her instincts kicked in and she made a decision that she hoped she wouldn't regret. "Call Dr. Hart and tell him I need him in here."

The tech gave her a nod and she entered the room. As Devon walked through the OR doors, she could see that the place was in total chaos as the anesthesiologist and two nurses were trying to contain the young patient, who was now shaking from head to toe, partially covered in a blue drape.

She looked for the doctor who should have been the one handling this emergency and couldn't believe what she found. Standing at the back of the room, Dr. Morgan had his arms crossed in front of his sterile gown as if he was patiently waiting for the rest of the staff to handle this emergency so that he could begin his surgery. Did he really think that they were going to continue with it?

"Let me help," Devon said as she moved to the head of the table and helped secure the boy's head.

"Thanks. I need to reverse the anesthesia and give him a dose of diazepam while we try to figure out what happened here." Devon didn't miss the scathing look the anesthesiologist gave Dr. Morgan.

"Reverse the anesthesia?" Dr. Morgan said from the back of the room. "If you'd already given him the diazepam, we could have been halfway through the surgery by now. Give it to him now and let me get started."

"He's been seizing like this for the past five minutes. There's no way that I'm going to leave him under the anesthesia," said one of the nurses indignantly. Devon looked over at her and was surprised to find that it was Rachel who had spoken up. She was a nurse who worked as a vendor representative and observed all the surgeries that their surgical devices were involved in, and Devon had liked the woman from the moment she'd met her. Then, as if needing the support, Rachel looked over at Devon. Though Devon didn't have all the facts that she needed to determine a cause for these seizures, anybody could see that the operation couldn't continue. Besides, the anesthesiologist had the right not to continue with the surgery at this point.

"Does the patient have a history of seizures?" she asked.

"It wasn't noted in his history," the anesthesiologist said. "And he didn't say anything about being on any seizure medications when I asked."

Because it was part of her job to help handle any issues that came up between the anesthesiologist department and the surgeons, she decided to be more tactful than she actually wanted to be with this particular surgeon.

"If this patient has a history of seizures, the anesthesia drugs could have lowered his seizure threshold, causing this issue. You have to agree that it's in the patient's best interest that we hold off on this surgery for now." Even as Devon had begun, she could see Dr. Morgan was going to argue with her. Not that it was going to change anything. She knew this whole room agreed with her and the anesthesiologist that the operation needed to be canceled.

"You're just a nurse. You can't make those decisions. I'm ordering you to give him the diazepam and let me do my job," Dr. Morgan said, his voice as sour as his words. The man really did need to go back to physician charm school and learn how to talk to people.

"You can't talk to her that way," Rachel objected, surprising Devon again. The look she gave Dr. Morgan said she was ready to go to war against him right then and there.

"She's not *just* a nurse. She's a nurse with a good head on her shoulders, and she's also absolutely right," Michael said from the door as he walked into the room toward the patient on the table.

Fortunately, while she'd been trying to reason with Dr. Morgan, the anesthesiologist had been reversing the anesthesia and pushing the IV diazepam. The boy's body finally relaxed and the seizures eased off.

"He's responding to the medication," she told Michael with relief, "but it was a grand mal seizure. We can't continue the surgery. He needs to be transferred to a hospital so he can be observed and have a neurologist consulted."

"I agree," Michael said, then turned to the

circulating RN. "Call nine-one-one and ask for transport. Tell them we have a young man who has just experienced a seizure on the operating table before the surgery had begun."

"Wait just a minute," Dr. Morgan said. For the first time, the man stepped up to the table where his patient was lying. "You can't do that. I'm the patient's surgeon."

"That's fine," Michael said. "You can handle the transport then and call the emergency room and give your report to the doctor there. But first, I think it would be best if you and I go inform the patient's mother what just happened."

"I don't need you to go with me to talk to my patient's family," Dr. Morgan said. Then, without even giving his patient a glance, he ripped off his sterile gown, dropped it on the floor, and stormed out of the room.

CHAPTER TEN

MICHAEL LOOKED UP when Devon stepped into his office. No one would have known by looking at her that she'd just led the team through a stressful incident in the operating room. Her scrubs were spotless and her hair, which had been pulled back into a high ponytail, seemed to bounce as she walked toward him. If not for the dark circles under her eyes, she'd be picture-perfect.

"You wanted to see me?" she asked. She might have looked okay, but the slight tremor in her voice said she had been just as affected as the rest of the operating team.

"I wanted to thank you for everything you did in the OR today. I can't believe a doctor would pull something like that. Having a patient hold back information is the same as falsifying information as far as I'm concerned." He'd already sent an email to Steve Morgan stating that his rights to perform surgery at the surgical center had been canceled. And he was also reporting the doctor to the board of medicine, now that he had learned exactly how ethically incompetent the man was turning out to be.

It was only when the ambulance had arrived and they had brought the boy's mother back to see him that it had come out that Dr. Morgan had told the mother and son that they shouldn't mention the boy's seizure history because it would keep him from having the surgery in an outpatient center. Since her son hadn't had a seizure since he was a child, she'd never considered that it would be a problem. They were lucky the teenager had recovered as quickly as he had.

"I talked to the boy's mother and he's doing well. They expect him to be discharged tomorrow after the neurologist sees him." She shook her head. "Apparently, the ER doctor had a lot of questions for them once they got there. According to the mother, he seemed to have as much trouble as we did with the surgeon's actions. I have to say, you handled Dr. Morgan even better than I thought you would."

"I don't know when I've been as angry at a coworker as I am with Steve right now. I appreciate you helping to cool down the situation. See, I knew hiring you was a good idea," he teased gently.

"But do you still feel that way after finding out about Conner? I know I was wrong to take the job without telling you about him first. If you feel that it could be a problem with us working together, I'd understand."

She looked away from him, and he knew he couldn't be angry with her any longer, no matter that he still didn't understand her decision. He stood, then went over to his office door and shut it, before going back to his desk.

"Can you please sit down so we can talk," he said, motioning to the chair in front of him. "And, no, I don't think we're going to have any problem working together. This isn't about the job."

He waited until she took a seat, though he noticed she sat on the edge with her hands clasped in her lap.

"Is this about the kiss?" he asked. "Is that why all of a sudden you're so nervous around me?"

She opened her mouth and then shut it and he had no doubts that she had been about to deny it.

He understood how she felt. He'd been thinking about it since the moment he'd left her. There had been something different about that kiss from all the other ones they'd shared before. But then everything he felt for Devon was totally different from anything he'd ever felt before. Holding Devon in his arms had felt so right, as if he had finally found exactly where he belonged. It had been as if he'd come home. It had been so long since he'd felt that way. He'd lost that feeling when his parents had been killed. The only personal connection he'd felt since then had been with his brother, but it wasn't the same.

Devon cleared her throat and crossed her arms. "I don't think your office is the place to discuss this. Do you?"

Leaning back in his chair, he looked at the woman who'd just taken on a surgeon without any fear, yet here she was afraid to discuss something as simple as a kiss. Not that he really thought that this particular kiss had been that simple. It had actually been very complicated. And now, it appeared to have the power to complicate things here, in his surgical center. "So we can both agree that there will be no talking about kisses in the workplace. What about the actual kissing? Is that allowed?"

Devon's cheeks turned the color of soft pink roses and Michael couldn't help but laugh. "You know I'm kidding you. If you don't want to discuss the kiss, that's fine. But you said you wanted us to be honest with each other and I can honestly say that I enjoyed that kiss very much."

"Will you be serious for a moment," Devon

said as she stood and gave him a look that would have put the fear into any seven-year-old boy. Fortunately, he was no longer seven.

"Okay, I won't mention it again. Not at work. But seriously, Devon. If you have a problem with anything between us, whether it's Conner or anything else, I want you to talk to me about it."

Her body relaxed as she stood there in front of him. "You know I will. Didn't you just see the way I handled Dr. Morgan? I have no problem speaking my mind."

After she left, Michael ignored the stack of paperwork on his desk, unable to make himself deal with it. It was much more fun to spar with Devon. If everything went well, he'd be able to hand off all of this to someone else soon, so that he could have more time to spend with Conner and Devon. It seemed like he had spent his whole life content to work toward that next big goal.

Now, he had something even more important in his life. He had a son. The fact that Devon came with the son could be complicated, though. Already, that they were feeling this attraction for each other was causing problems. He couldn't deny that he enjoyed being with her. But he worried how it would affect Conner if things between Michael and Devon went too far and then went sour.

Boys were protective of their mothers. He'd been protective of his, yet still he'd lost her because of a drunk driver. Michael knew the pain that came with losing a parent. Conner had already lost his father at a very young age. Conner would be even more protective of his mother now. And hurting Devon would hurt his son. Was he really willing to take that chance?

He thought about the kiss they'd shared. He might have teased Devon about it, but the truth was that he'd felt more passion in those few moments than he'd felt for years. There was something about her that drew him to her. He'd felt it that night on the beach, and he'd felt it the night at the hotel. Both times, other events had interceded and they'd gone their separate ways. Now, there was no possibility of the two of them doing that. They were tied together for life because of their son.

And he was already afraid that any plan he might come up with to ignore this need that they felt for each other was already doomed to fail.

For the next two weeks, Devon found herself and Conner spending each night eating dinner with Michael. On nights when they ate at Devon's place, she and Michael would share the cleanup of the kitchen and getting Conner to bed. Afterward, they'd spend an hour or so talking out on the porch together. They talked about work or something going on in Conner's life. They talked about their town and the people they knew there. But not once did Michael bring up the subject of telling Conner about Michael being his biological father. He seemed to understand that Conner needed time to get to know him better and to get used to him being a part of his life. He also made no attempt to bring up the subject of the kiss they'd shared. And he'd made no move to kiss her again.

While Devon appreciated his understanding about Conner, she had to admit that she was missing his kisses. Somehow, him not kissing her made her even more aware of his presence whenever they were alone. It was like she had some ticking bomb inside her that was just waiting for one touch from him to set it off. It was taking all her strength not to reach out and touch him, and see exactly how much damage the two of them could do to each other.

So while they'd sat on the porch, each sipping a glass of the wine Michael had brought over the night before, all she could think about was this need for him that she could feel building inside of her.

"There's something I want to ask you," Michael said as he set his glass down. "I don't have to have an answer now, though I hope your answer will be yes. It's something that I think would be good for all three of us."

Suddenly her mind went into overdrive, leaving memories of those kisses she was dreaming about behind, and jumping way too fast for Devon into thoughts of a proposal. Her hand came up to her chest as her heart began to thump too fast. Her, marry Michael?

She could see how a marriage between the two of them would be good for their son, but she'd done that once before. If she ever married again, it would need to be for the right reasons. She would never marry again unless she was in love. She'd been lucky her marriage to Zach had been such a good one. They had been friends, and later, lovers, but she wouldn't go into a marriage like that again.

"Are you okay?" Michael asked. He got up from his chair and bent down in front of her. "Are you having chest pain? Should I call nine-one-one?"

She couldn't speak. Her breaths came too fast and her ears were filled with a roaring sound. Was this what a panic attack felt like?

Maybe she'd been obsessing over his kisses recently, but she wasn't ready for a proposal. She placed her hands in her lap and, with the calmest voice she could manage, said, "No. I'm fine. But maybe it would be best if we waited before discussing anything else tonight."

He sat there in front of her for a few more moments. Then, after studying her face for several seconds and appearing to be satisfied that she wasn't going to pass out, he stood. "I don't want to rush you, but the game is next week and I don't want my friend to hold the tickets for us if you don't want to go. And if we are going, then I'll need to reserve a plane for us."

Her mind went blank. For a moment, it just stopped processing information. It was like the blood flowing up to her brain had taken a vacation and headed for her toes. Her thoughts weren't just scrambled, they had simply disappeared. It took a moment for her brain to come back online and she began to realize that she had made a grave mistake in thinking that Michael had wanted to ask her to marry him.

"A plane? Tickets for a game?" she asked, her voice higher than usual.

"Yes. It's in Tampa, so it will be a short flight, and the game is at one, so we won't be too late getting back. I get these offers all the time from the people I used to play with. I normally turn them down, but I think Conner would really enjoy seeing a live game."

"I'm sure he would," she said. The feeling was finally coming back into her arms and legs, and she was even beginning to see some humor in the situation, though she would never share it with Michael. She was just glad she hadn't made any more of a fool of herself than she had already. "How about I get back to you in the morning?"

"That's fine," Michael said, then went on to change the subject to something that had happened in the operating room that day.

He appeared totally oblivious to where her mind had gone earlier, which was a good thing for her. A proposal? She'd really thought Michael Hart was actually going to ask her to marry him? The mere thought was ridiculous.

But when he left that night, she couldn't help but feel disappointed once again when he made no attempt to kiss her good-night.

CHAPTER ELEVEN

As they made their way into the fancy suite inside the football stadium, Devon was glad that she'd taken the time to dress up a little for the game. She'd seen pictures of all the celebrity guests and famous football players' wives dressed in short dresses and boots, but she hadn't gone that far. Instead, she'd worn her nicest pair of skinny black jeans and had splurged on a new team jersey, as it had been Michael's team before he'd been injured. The only thing the least bit different from what she normally would have worn to a game were the sequins that decorated the team's name and the heeled boots she wore.

She thought she looked quite nice until they were ushered into a room filled with women dressed in clothes that would have cost her a month's income. If the private jet and the limousine ride from the airport hadn't been intimidating enough, this was almost mind-blowing. She was just a nurse from a little beach town.

What was she supposed to talk about with these people?

"I'll be right back," Michael said as a man waved to him from down a set of steps where the seats faced a large window.

"Mom, you're squeezing my hand," Conner complained from beside her as he pulled against the tight hold she had on his hand.

She looked down at her son and let go of him. But when he started to step away from her, she put her hand on his shoulder. "Stay with me until Michael finds out where we're supposed to be seated."

"But can I go ask him if I can get one of those sodas over there?" he asked, pointing to where a large glass bowl filled with ice and drinks sat in the middle of a table draped in a white linen tablecloth.

"Of course you can have a soda, if it's okay with your mom," a woman said as she stepped toward them.

"I'm Lily, Darek's wife." The woman's smile seemed genuine, though it was as bright as the teardrop diamonds hanging from her ears. "You must be Devon and Conner. Darek was so happy to hear that you were coming today. He's been trying to get Michael to a game for years."

Devon looked over to where Michael was surrounded by a group of men, all seeming happy to see him. Some of the men she could picture as former players. Those were the large men who were in their late thirties or early forties, but she could tell they still worked out in the gym. Then there were others who seemed to be guests, like her and Michael. Michael had explained that Darek was the friend who'd invited them to the game, but that was all he'd told her. "It's nice to be here. Conner has been excited all week. He's big into football even though he's only seven. Michael is one of his coaches."

"And you? Are you a football fan or are you just a Michael fan?" another woman asked as she stepped up beside Lily. Devon looked at the woman, unsure how she was supposed to respond.

"Ignore Janie," Lily said, rolling her eyes at the woman.

"I guess you could say I'm both," Devon said, answering the woman even though the question seemed rude. "I've known him since I was a kid. I watched him play in high school. And now, I work for him. We're friends. Just friends."

She swallowed when Janie continued to stare at her. The woman looked Devon up and down before turning away and walking off to join another group.

"What was that about?" Devon asked Lily when she was sure the woman was far enough away that she couldn't hear her.

"Old news. She had a thing for Michael back in the day, but she's harmless. Michael never had any interest in her," Lily said.

Devon looked back at Janie and saw that she had quickly made her way over to the men, and now had her arms wrapped around Michael's neck in a hug. Devon's eyes narrowed and she had to hold herself back from walking over and pulling the woman off him.

"So just friends, huh?" Lily said. Devon looked back at her and saw her eyes sparkling with mischief. "Don't worry, your secret's safe with me. The only thing I care about is that you've somehow gotten Michael to come join us, which will make my husband a happy man tonight."

Devon didn't know what to say, so she looked around for Conner. She was surprised to see that there were other children playing games at a corner table. She'd been so busy checking out the men and women that she hadn't seen them. But Conner wasn't with the other children. Instead, he had walked down the steps to where the fanciest stadium seats she had ever seen lined a glass window that looked out into the stadium.

"Excuse me," Devon said, then headed over to where Conner stood with his face as close to the window as it was possible to be. She started to pull out a tissue from her purse to wipe his fingerprints off the glass, then decided against it.

"Wow, that's a great view, isn't it?" she asked as she stepped up to the window beside him.

"This is amazing," Conner said without taking his eyes off the field.

"What do you think?" Michael said, coming up behind them. "Are you ready for some football, Conner?"

A moment later, the teams took the field and Conner began to clap. An intercom system came on and almost everyone started to take their seats. Michael held his hand out to Devon, and she took it. But after he'd led them to their seats, he let go.

One team kicked off and the game began. In moments, the excitement of the game had filled the room. There were screams of celebration and moans of disappointment as the two teams battled on the field. By the end of the first quarter, Devon had become as vocal as the rest of the group. When Michael's former team went for a touchdown on the fourth down with one yard to the goal, everyone in the room was on their feet. As the team's offensive line pushed forward and the quarterback dived over them to score the first touchdown of the game, the room exploded with screams.

Michael turned to her, and before she knew it, she was clasped in his arms and lifted off the ground. When Michael put her on her feet, Conner was in front of them laughing at her. "Mom, why is your face so red?"

"Because the team made a touchdown, of course," Devon said and then looked up at Michael, who was laughing along with her son. Then they all took their seats to prepare for the kicker's attempt at an extra point.

For the rest of the first half, Devon found it hard to pay attention to what was happening on the field. She was wound too tight after the hug she'd shared with Michael. It seemed every few minutes Michael would touch her hand and point out something on the field. Once, he'd rested his arm across the back of her seat and she'd been afraid to lean back in case his arm touched her shoulder. She'd begun to accept the idea that Michael really wasn't interested in kissing her again. If only her body would accept it instead of reacting like some sex-starved idiot every time he touched her!

As soon as it was halftime, Devon excused herself and found the restroom. After washing her hands, she looked into the mirror and saw that her face did have a pink flush to it. She couldn't help but wonder if Michael was playing some game with her. Since the night he'd kissed her, he'd made no move toward her for anything except having contact with Conner. Yes, the two of them were growing closer, as friends, while they got Conner used to having Michael around. Was he giving her all this attention today for his friends? No, he wasn't the type of man to need a woman on his arm for his ego. So what was going on?

By the time she walked back into the suite, she'd decided that she would have to speak to Michael the next time they were alone. Even though they were spending their time together for Conner, they needed to be careful that he didn't get the wrong idea about the relationship between the two of them.

Seeing Michael across the room in deep conversation with a group of people, and Conner in the corner where the other kids were playing, she walked over to the window and looked down on the field, where the halftime performance was just finishing up.

"Devon?" a man said as he joined her. "I'm Darek. Darek Roberts."

It only took a moment to put together where

she had heard the name. Lily's husband had been one of the two tackles that had slammed into Michael during the last game of his career. "I know you," Devon said. "You're one of the men who tackled Michael the night he was injured."

"I'm afraid so," Darek said. The man shook his head, and his eyes dropped to the ground. "I've relived that moment too many times to count."

Devon could tell the man's sorrow for what had happened was real. She'd watched that play more times than she wanted to count, too. There had been no ill intent on either of the men's part. "It was an accident. I'm sure Michael doesn't blame you."

The man looked up at her. "Michael is one of a kind. Even when they were loading him up on a stretcher to carry him off the field, he was assuring me that it wasn't my fault. That didn't make it any easier to bear when I found out just how bad he was injured, though. I think maybe it made it harder. The day they announced that he wasn't going to be able to play again was one of the worst days of my life."

"But you were on another team," Devon said. Seeing this six-foot-plus man who was the size of a refrigerator looking like he'd lost his best friend was almost painful. "You were just doing your job by stopping the play. I read the papers. No one blamed you or the other player."

"Didn't matter if they blamed us. We knew how hard Michael had worked to get into professional football, because we'd done the work, too. Having it all end for him right then was painful for all of us," Darek said.

"He told me that the two of you are friends, so I know there's no ill will on his part." Though she couldn't deny that she'd been angry with the men who'd caused Michael's injuries when it had first happened, she'd accepted it as something that none of the players had any control over. The anger had faded enough for her to think about it clearly. It was just part of the game and a risk that all the players took when they stepped on the field. "And look what he's done with his life. I work with him now and I can honestly tell you that he's a great doctor."

"I know. He did my knee replacement not long after he passed his boards. He thought I let him do it out of guilt, but that wasn't it."

"Then why?" she asked, knowing this man could have had any surgeon he wanted do the operation.

"Because I knew if he'd put in half the work to be a doctor as he had to be the kind of quarterback he used to be, then he would do an excellent job." The man looked down at his right knee, lifted it, and then began to swing it back and forth. "Like I said, an excellent job."

Devon smiled at this giant of a man who'd mowed down players on the field and realized he was just a great big teddy bear. "I'm glad to hear it."

"But that wasn't what I wanted to talk to you about. I came over here to tell you just how much I appreciate you getting him here today."

"He invited me," Devon said, confused about why the man thought she should take credit for Michael being there.

"I've been inviting him for years, ever since I quit playing and joined this group of broken-down ex-players. But he'd always come up with some reason why he couldn't make it. I have to believe you have something to do with why he's here now."

Devon looked around the room and found that Michael had left the group of men and was now bent down talking to Conner. "I think it's more likely that it's my son who got him here today."

Darek looked over to where Michael and Conner were deep in what looked like a very serious conversation, then shook his head. "Maybe so, but I think you had a lot more to do with it than you think."

The halftime clock ticked down and everyone returned to their seats as the teams returned to the field. For the rest of the game, Michael and Conner had their heads together as they discussed the players and the plays. Devon told herself that she wasn't disappointed when Michael didn't touch her again for the rest of the game. She was so confused, not only by Michael's actions, but also by her own reactions. She knew that Michael's interest needed to be on Conner and he had always had the power to focus on what was important in his life. He'd done it with his football career and later his medical career. Yet a part of her, a part she was ashamed to admit to, wanted some of that focus to be on her, even though she knew that was wrong.

Sitting up in her seat, she forced herself to pay attention to the field. Just then, the other team scored a touchdown, tying up the game. There were moans in the room, and one celebratory cheer from the lone home-team fan. The tension in the room was high and Devon found herself caught up in the game once again.

Michael looked over to where Conner lay curled up in his seat asleep as they flew the short distance back to the Florida panhandle.

"He doesn't look very comfortable," he said to Devon, who sat on his other side.

"He's fine," Devon said as she leaned forward and looked over at her son. "Normally, after staying up this late I'd have a hard time getting him up for school in the morning, but he's so stoked about that football Darek had all the players sign for him that I'm sure he'll pop right up."

Michael didn't want to say anything about the signing of the football. It would seem trivial to most people. It was just normal that Conner would ask for his signature, too. But maybe Devon needed to know that it had bothered him and why.

"What's wrong?" Devon asked shrewdly.

"I don't know how to explain this," he said. "It's just when Conner asked me to sign that football for him, I couldn't do it."

He wasn't sure how to explain that when his son had looked at him hoping to get an autograph from his "Coach Hart," for the first time he'd felt as if he was deceiving Conner.

"I understand," she said. "Having Conner calling you 'Coach Hart' now that you know he's your father feels wrong to me, too."

"So what do we do about it?" he asked. He knew what he wanted to do. He wanted to wake his son up and tell him the truth, but he knew that wasn't the right thing to do. "Do you think we should consult a counselor?"

"You mean like a family counselor? I hadn't considered that. I don't know. Maybe we just need to give it a little more time. You know he's crazy about you. It's bound to be a shock, though. But he's a strong kid. Just give us a couple more weeks of him getting used to you being around and then we can tell him."

"Together?" he asked.

Devon hesitated for a moment then looked back over to where Conner slept. Michael wasn't sure he agreed with them waiting another two weeks, but he did know that she only had their son's best interests in mind.

Finally, she looked up at him. "Okay. We'll tell him, together."

Later that night, after they'd arrived back at Devon's home and had gotten Conner into bed, the two of them stepped out on the porch to say good-night. Michael had made a point of keeping things light between them for the last two weeks. There had been no good-night kisses since the first one they'd shared. He was doing his best to keep his focus on his son.

Then he'd seen her in those fitted jeans and heeled boots, her hair trailing down her shoulders and her lips painted a bright red to match her jersey, and all his resolve had begun to melt. He'd known that this was bound to happen. The pull between them was too strong. But after sitting beside her at the game and then in the plane, it had been all he could do to keep his hands off her. He'd come up with reasons to show her something on the field just so that he could touch her hand. He'd held up longer than he could be expected to. It was time to throw caution to the wind. And he was about to throw it as far as he could. He just hoped that she was ready to receive it.

"So how was this for a first date?" he asked, hoping to throw her off guard.

"This was a date?" she asked, her eyes narrowing at him. "I'm pretty sure I didn't agree to this being a date."

"I asked you to the game and you agreed to go. Therefore, it was a date." He gave her his best smile and when those lips that he had been fantasizing about all day turned up, he knew he had her. "And as we have both now agreed that this was our first date, it only seems right that we end it with a kiss."

He bent his head to kiss her and was surprised when her arms instinctively curled around his neck and drew him closer. Then her lips parted and he lost it. His tongue touched hers and his hands slid up her neck and into her hair, holding her mouth to his as he plunged deep inside. She tasted so good on his tongue, but it wasn't enough. He wanted to taste all of her. He pulled away and was rewarded with her protest. Then he moved his lips to her collarbone, just above the neckline of her jersey, and began to work his way up. After he reached the top of her cheek, he moved to the back of her ear. Her body shuddered and her breasts rubbed against his chest. He'd never forgotten how responsive she was when he'd kissed her there the night they'd spent together. Nor had he forgotten just how her responsiveness had affected him. If they didn't stop soon, they were going to be putting on a show for the whole neighborhood. They had to find somewhere new to kiss.

He pulled his mouth away then rested his chin on top of her head, which she leaned against his chest. They both were breathless and maybe a little unsteady, so they clung together for several moments.

"I have to say that was the best first-date kiss I've ever had," he said between breaths. From the way his heart was pounding, he didn't think he would have survived if it had been any better.

After a moment, Devon lifted her head from

his chest. Her deep green eyes were bright, though he knew she had to be tired after the long day they'd had.

"I guess it was pretty good," she said, smiling up at him. At that moment, while she was teasing him, she was once again the girl he'd known as Sunshine.

Then her smile turned to a frown. "I don't understand. You've acted like you didn't want to kiss me, or even touch me, for the last two weeks. What gives?"

He saw the hurt in her eyes and knew he had messed up. "I'm sorry. I admit, I've been trying to keep things…less intimate between the two of us. I was afraid of what might happen if Conner started to think of us as more than friends. I don't want to confuse or hurt him."

"Okay," she said slowly. "I understand that. I'm worried about that, too. I lived in a home where men came and went on a weekly basis. I would never do that to my son. That doesn't mean that I'm never going to have another relationship, though."

The last thing he wanted to do was listen to her talk about having a relationship with any man but him. "I don't understand. You're planning on hiding these relationships?"

"Not hiding, as much as being discreet. My

life would have been a lot better if my mother had been more discreet. Maybe when Conner's older and if I have a serious relationship it would be okay for him to know, but I don't see why right now he would need to know anything about that part of my life."

"So are you suggesting that it's okay for the two of us to have a relationship as long as Conner doesn't know?" he asked. Even though he understood her reasoning, he didn't know how he would feel about being her secret fling.

She tilted her head to the side and looked him up and down, a playful smile on her lips. "How about I think about it and let you know?"

Laughing, he stepped away and started down the steps. "Good night, Sunshine."

In the darkness, he heard her laughing behind him. "Good night, Mickey."

CHAPTER TWELVE

MONDAY MORNING CAME too soon for Devon, so when Conner had woken her, his eyes bright with the excitement of taking his new signed football to school, her mood had not been the best. She was tired and cranky. And she knew exactly who was to blame.

She'd tried her best to sleep, but her mind had refused to shut down and her body had refused to go back into that no-sex mode it had been in for the last year. Michael admitting that he had purposely cooled things down between them because he was afraid of hurting Conner had just made her want him more.

The two of them had been concentrating on him getting to know Conner better and he'd made no effort to take things any further between him and Devon. And while a part of her had been disappointed in that, she had known that he was concentrating on his relationship with Conner.

Then…pow! He'd changed everything between the two of them again with another good-night kiss. But she hadn't let him get away with it as easily as he had thought. She'd called him on it. He couldn't keep going back and forth, from hot to cold, whenever he wanted. His concerns were legitimate, but they could be worked around.

Not that she wasn't nervous about where things could go wrong between them. She'd never admit it to him, but even after all these years, she remembered feeling so alone as she'd waited for that phone call from him that had never come.

Only this time, things would be different. Neither of them was looking for more than a good time together. They had an attraction that needed to be burned off. That was all.

Feeling better about things, she climbed out of bed and began her day.

An hour later, she arrived at work and found two people, a woman and a man, waiting for her at the front desk from the state health-care agency. As they introduced themselves and explained why they were there, she tried to make sense of it all.

"So someone put in a complaint against the surgical center?" she asked. She'd been involved in several accreditations over the years, but she'd never dealt directly with a complaint being filed.

"Yes. We actually received a complaint from a doctor who practices here." The woman handed Devon a very official piece of paper.

Devon read through the complaint and saw the patient's name listed. James Waters. The elderly man who owned the bakery, who'd had the atrial fibrillation. She should have known that Dr. Morgan would be behind this. After being denied surgical rights, he'd decided to make a complaint about the surgical center? He couldn't have thought this out very well. If he had, he would have known that this would look bad for him.

She looked at her watch, then glanced down at the surgery schedule on her desk. Michael was in surgery. She'd have to handle this and inform him later.

"I'm glad you brought this to our attention. Now, how can I help you with this investigation?" Devon asked them.

An hour later, the recovery nurses that had taken care of Mr. Waters had all been interviewed, and the chart had been reviewed. Devon had been the first to be interviewed, since she was specifically named on the complaint. She'd explained that she had been the one to request another doctor for the patient when Dr. Morgan had failed to return the nurses' calls. When the investigators had questioned why she thought the doctor hadn't called back, she'd been honest. "I can't tell you the exact reason, but it seemed to me that he felt he had done his part and we needed to handle whatever came up after the surgery. Which is exactly what ended up happening."

While the investigators didn't make a lot of comments before they left, the looks Devon had seen pass between them told her that the evidence pointed to the problem being Steve Morgan and not the care that the surgical center's staff had given the patient.

She knew that Michael saw patients in the afternoon after his surgeries, so she texted him that she had something she needed to talk to him about. When she received a text inviting her to have lunch with him in his office, she messaged her agreement. When he replied that he would handle the food, she sent him back a smiley emoji and realized she was smiling just as widely as the expressive emblem. She was in so much trouble.

By the time she got to his office, Michael was waiting for her with a delivery bag of food on his desk. "You might want to let me tell you about this first, before we eat," she warned him.

She handed him a copy of the complaint. "You don't have to worry about it, though. I've already handled it."

His eyes seemed to race over the paper, while his hands tightened and his knuckles turned white. "Tell me."

So as she unpacked the delivery bag she told him about the investigators arriving that morning and how they'd very thoroughly interviewed the staff. "I'm not sure what he was trying to accomplish, but he had to know that it would make him look bad when they investigated his complaint."

"I'm not sure he even believes he did anything wrong. I appreciate how you handled this. I just hope he's not going to make any more trouble for us. Maybe when the investigators go back to him with their findings, he'll realize that it's best to just move on."

For a few moments, they busied themselves with their sandwiches while Devon went more in-depth concerning the investigation. Though she hated that there had been an investigation, it had taken her mind off what had happened between them the night before.

It wasn't until Devon began to clean up her

food wrappers that Michael changed the subject from work to something more personal. "I thought, since our first date went so well, that maybe we should give a second date a try."

She stopped by the trash can and put her hands on her hips. "Just so there's no misunderstanding this time. You are actually inviting me out on a date?"

She watched as he leaned back in his chair and gave her that ridiculously charming smile of his. She would bet money that Dr. Michael Hart had never had to attend a physician's charm school. All he had to do was smile at his patients, at least his female patients, to make them happy.

"There's a sunset cruise that leaves out of the Destin Harbor Saturday night. We could drive down that afternoon and either drive back home that night or spend the night there."

Devon wasn't sure what to say. From the way things had ended the night before, she wasn't completely surprised by the invitation for a second date. But spending a night together? That would be moving their relationship forward faster than what she was prepared for. "The sunset cruise sounds lovely, but I don't know about spending the night. Conner is supposed to go fishing with Max and his dad Saturday afternoon. I'm not sure if he's staying overnight, though, so I'll have to check."

"It's okay if you don't want to stay the night. I'm not trying to rush you into anything," Michael said.

Devon couldn't deny that the thought of spending the night with Michael was very tempting and knew that tonight would be another sleepless night.

By the end of their second date, Michael was pretty sure it had been a success. The yacht hadn't been overcrowded. The music hadn't been too loud. The meal had been delicious. And the company had been the best. They'd almost missed the beautiful sunset because they'd been so busy talking that they hadn't noticed when everyone else had left the dining room. It had been the waiter who had reminded them—he'd explained that there was a small patio off the back of the dining room where they could see the sunset without the other diners being present. Michael had left the man a hefty tip before he'd escorted Devon outside.

Fall had finally come to the Florida panhandle, though there was very little evidence. The daytime temperatures were still warm, but at night they fell down into the sixties. As they stepped outside, the wind off the water caught Devon's hair and blew it back against him. Scents of strawberries and lemons drifted around him, stirring something inside him. He'd begun to recognize her scent and found himself missing it when she was away from him.

"It's beautiful," Devon said as she leaned against the boat's railing. "All that pink and purple mixed with the dark blue and the bright gold from the last rays of the sun. I don't stop and enjoy things like this like I use to. I used to walk along the beach every night and watch the sunset."

"I remember. I used to look out my window and see you there. I didn't understand why you did that then." He came up behind her and slipped his arms around her waist, pulling her against him. She was wearing a pretty sleeveless dress made out of a soft material that seemed to float in the breeze. A gust came up and she shivered in his arms, the motion causing his body to tighten and harden. At that moment, he was so glad he'd given up on trying to keep his hands off her.

"That's because the only thing you had eyes for then was a football," Devon teased.

"I had other interests, too. Why do you think I looked out my window? I knew when to expect you."

She turned in his arms and looked up at him. "Really?"

"Yes, really. I thought you were the prettiest girl in school back then." He bent down and kissed the tip of her nose. "Now, I think you're the most beautiful woman I've ever known."

The smile she gave him told him that she thought he was teasing her. Why couldn't she see herself as he did? Maybe because he'd hurt her before? That thought stung. He'd made her feel unwanted. He never wanted Devon to feel that way again. Instead, he wanted her to understand what it was that he saw when he looked at her. He wanted her to know how much he wanted her. So he kissed her.

When he lifted his mouth, he murmured, "I love the way your lips feel and the way they smile whenever you talk about Conner."

He kissed her nose, then said, "I love the way your pretty little nose twitches right before you let off a most unladylike sneeze."

She laughed and he kissed each one of her cheeks. "I love the way your cheeks turn pink when you're excited or embarrassed. Just like they're doing now."

She tried to bury her face in his chest, but he wouldn't let her. "And I love those beautiful green eyes of yours. They've seen so much sadness, but they still manage to sparkle with laughter when Conner is telling you a story about his day at school."

Then he smiled down at her. "Did I tell you how much I love those lips of yours?"

"I can't seem to remember if you did or not," she said, her lips turning up in a flirtatious smile. "Maybe you should show me."

And so he did.

Devon shivered as Michael drove them home. The night had been magical and she didn't want it to end. Still, she was unsure if she should take things further with Michael this soon. But whether she should or not, there was no denying that she wanted to spend the night with him. Just like always, she hadn't wanted the kisses they'd shared on the cruise to end.

As they turned down the road that would take both of them home, her to her place, and him to his own home, even though Conner was sleeping over at Max's, she made her decision. She couldn't deny that she had made some decisions in her life that she regretted, but she couldn't see how this one night could hurt anything. It was just one night.

But wasn't that what she'd told herself the night she'd spent with Michael and then come home pregnant? That was exactly what had happened. And wasn't that the reason she'd made a trip up to the store right out of town by the interstate last night, and purchased a box of condoms? She'd wanted to be prepared for whatever might happen tonight.

Making up her mind, she patted her purse where the box had been safely tucked away, then looked over at Michael. "Do you feel up to a glass of wine at your place?"

The look he gave her was smoldering-hot and she knew he understood that her question wasn't really about the wine. "Are you sure?"

She swallowed her doubt back and put on a smile she hoped was more confident than she felt. It had been a long time, over eight years, since she'd done anything like this. It had been well over a year since she'd had any physical contact with anyone. Her body had become hypersensitive since the first kisses they'd shared on her porch. Just thinking about that night had her body humming with a need she knew she couldn't deny any longer.

She nodded her head, then managed to say the words. "Yes, I'm sure."

Michael's hands tightened on the steering wheel. "I appreciate the fact that you didn't mention this earlier. Otherwise, I might not have been able to make it back here safely."

She couldn't help but laugh at his admission. "I guess it's a good thing that I didn't mention that I was carrying a box of condoms in my purse all night."

"If I'd known that, we definitely wouldn't have made it out your front door," he said as he pulled into his driveway and turned off the truck. He opened his door, then made a grab for her purse before jumping out and running over to her side of the vehicle. She had just opened the door when he grabbed her and flipped her over his shoulder.

"Michael, what are you doing?" she said between laughs.

He took the stairs two at a time, laughing as he wrapped one arm securely around her legs and patted her bottom with the other. Devon couldn't believe that he had gone all caveman on her, but she had to admit, she liked it.

He set her down at the door, making sure she was steady before punching in the alarm code and opening the door.

"I didn't realize you needed that glass of wine so badly," she joked as she walked into his living room. She looked back to find him still standing at the door, her purse hanging from his shoulder. Oh, how she wished she had a picture of this strong, masculine man wearing her glittery gold purse.

"I don't think I've ever needed anything…no, make that I've never needed anyone as badly as I need you right now." As he walked toward her, he opened his arms.

The laughter they'd shared a few minutes was gone. There was only desire in his eyes now. Desire for her. She walked into his arms and just rested there for a moment. Nothing had ever felt so perfect.

Then he kissed her and all thoughts left her brain. His lips seemed to devour hers. She molded herself against him, needing to get as close as possible. She wanted to feel him inside her. Moving, stretching her, filling her.

"Where?" she asked, her head lifting as his lips ran up her skin from her collarbone to that sensitive spot behind her ear. Her breath caught and she arched into him. He was driving her crazy with her kisses, but she wanted more.

She looked around the room where a large sectional couch sat. That would never do. His lips had moved to the other side of her neck now, and were working their way back to where the neckline of her dress cut down to a point as his hands began to work on her buttons.

When his tongue skimmed across the top of her breasts, she decided to take things into her own hands, so to speak. Moving her hands between them, she ran her fingers across the front of his pants. He was long and steel-hard, and for a second, she forgot all about finding someplace more comfortable for them to share. If nothing else, there was the dining room table nearby. She had unbuckled his belt, popped the button off his pants, and began to lower his zipper when she felt her dress slip away, leaving her standing in a tiny pair of panties and a matching bra. Once again, she felt herself leave the floor as Michael gathered her up in his arms.

"You do have my purse, right?" she said as they topped the stairs and turned toward a room at the end of the hall.

"I wouldn't think of leaving it behind," he assured her.

He pushed the door open and placed Devon on her feet once again. His hand came up and tucked her hair behind her ears. She felt the tremble in his fingers as they ran down her cheek, and then between her breasts as he slid her bra off her shoulders. "I only want one promise from you. Tomorrow, when I wake up, I want you to be here beside me."

It was such a little thing to ask and she understood that he feared, like the first time they'd slept together, she would be gone the next morning. "I promise I'll still be here."

With that promise, she removed the rest of her clothes and watched as he removed his shirt and then his pants. A moment later they were stretched out on his bed, his strong arms holding her as he teased her with his mouth and hands. Her own hands and lips explored his body, discovering scars that she knew hadn't been there the last time they'd been bared to each other. Her hands slid lower, and she wrapped her hand around the thick length of him and guided it to her entrance. He slid inside her, and she thought that she'd explode from the pleasure of him being there, finally.

For a moment they just looked at each other and an irrational fear filled her until she saw the depth of longing in his eyes and remembered that it was the same longing she'd seen once before, which had convinced her that their act of lovemaking was more than just a physical thing between them.

Then he started moving and the only thing she knew was the pleasure of his body as it thrust inside of her. She felt the tension growing, spiraling with every thrust. His lips moved to that special spot behind her ear, then he whispered, “Sunshine, come for me.”

As if her body had been waiting for the command, her orgasm burst through her. He ground against her, each thrust prolonging her pleasure, until finally he reached his own release with a shout, and then the two of them sank deep down into the covers together.

She lay there beside him, her body sated while she tried to push down the fear she’d felt earlier when they were making love. She reminded herself that she wasn’t the same girl she’d been the last time she’d fallen under Michael’s spell. She’d grown up to become a woman. A woman who’d been through enough pain in her life. She’d told herself that she could have a relationship with a man without any expectations. And that probably would have worked with any other man except the one who was currently lying beside her.

CHAPTER THIRTEEN

MICHAEL WOKE TO find Devon beside him, shaking him. "Morning, Sunshine," he said, before rolling over on top of her to kiss her good morning.

"Morning is almost gone. I've got to get up." She laughed as he began to press kisses all over her face, then pushed against him and tried to wiggle out from between his arms. "I'm serious. I told Max's parents that I would pick Conner up before lunch. Besides, I have to do the grocery shopping and get clothes ready for the week. I should have been up a couple hours ago."

He loosened his hold and let her squeeze out from under him, enjoying the feel of her naked body against his, then got up himself. "Don't stress. We can do this."

"We? I'm going to be grocery shopping and doing laundry. I'm not sure how much help you're going to be," she said as she bent down and gathered the few clothes that had made it upstairs.

He had to pause for a moment and just take her in. At that moment, he felt like the luckiest man alive. He wanted to take her straight back to bed. Instead, he bent down and picked up his pants off the floor. He pulled out his keys and tossed them toward Devon. “Take my truck and go get changed. I’ll grab a shower and be ready by the time you get back. We can pick up Conner and go out for brunch.”

Not waiting for her to agree, he walked into the bathroom. A few moments later he heard his truck crank up. He looked into the mirror and saw that goofy smile that the media had always seemed to love. They didn’t know that most of the time, while he was fighting his way up the ranks in college, then winning the Claymont Trophy, and eventually playing professional football, that smile had been forced. But today, it was totally genuine. There was nothing that he’d rather do than spend the day doing all those everyday domestic chores with Devon and Conner.

Several hours later, when Michael looked over at Devon as they cleaned the kitchen, he was surprised to see just how fresh she still looked.

"I don't know how you do it. I was tired by the time we got finished with the groceries."

"Buying groceries would have gone a lot quicker if you and Conner hadn't decided to play games and keep putting those ridiculous items in my cart," Devon said tartly, taking the platter he'd just washed and drying it carefully. He still didn't understand why anyone would have dishes that couldn't be put in the dishwasher. "And between the two of you, I spent twice as much on groceries as I usually do."

"I tried to get you to let me pay." It had been the only disagreement they'd had that day and Michael still wasn't sure how he'd lost that argument. He had wanted to insist that it was his son that she was feeding, but with Conner beside him, he couldn't fight that battle.

"Let's not talk about it right now, okay?" Devon said as she moved between him and the cabinet where he'd just placed the last glass he'd dried. "Conner's in the shower and we have a few moments alone. Let's not waste them."

Michael placed his arms on the counter behind her and bent his head toward her. The kiss started off as playful, teasing, but it quickly heated up. Her arms circled his neck and he lifted her onto the countertop. Her legs opened to let him in closer and she wrapped them around his waist.

"What are you doing?" Conner asked from behind him.

Suddenly all the desire that had been coursing through Michael's body vanished in an instant.

Devon's legs fell from Michael's waist and her head dropped down to his chest. How was she supposed to explain to her son what he had just interrupted? She guessed she should be glad that he'd come in before things had gotten any more heated between her and Michael. She wanted to just stay there in Michael's arms and pretend that there wasn't anything unusual about her being plastered against her son's football coach's body. But she was the mom and she had to do what moms did a lot of the time. She had to improvise.

But first, she had to get Michael to let her go. Pushing against his chest, she managed to wiggle down between the cabinets and his firm body until her feet touched the floor and she stepped away from Michael. "Conner, what exactly is it you thought you saw?"

She knew Conner was very observant. That was why he was always asking questions. If he saw something that he didn't understand, he was going to ask questions until he figured it out. She just hoped this wasn't one of those times.

"I saw Coach Hart kissing you and it looked like you liked it." The look Conner gave her reminded her of that old black-and-white show when the husband would tell his wife that he had some explaining to do. "You're not supposed to be kissing."

"Uh, but sometimes people like to kiss," Michael said, coming to stand beside her.

"Mommies and daddies kiss. That's what you said, Mom," Conner said, then turned toward Michael. "Does that mean you're going to be my stepdad? There's a girl at school who says she's had three stepdads."

Michael looked at her and she could see that he thought this was the moment they'd been waiting for.

She took a deep breath and let it out. "Conner, I need to tell you something. It's about your dad. It might be hard for you to fully understand until you get older, but I want to tell you now. You see, Coach Hart isn't just your coach. He's your dad." Devon knew the moment the words came out of her mouth that she hadn't done this right. Her son would only have more questions from the lack of information she had given him.

"But my dad died," Conner said, the pain in

his voice stabbing her through her own heart. "You know that, Mom. He got sick. We went to see him at the hospital. Then Grandma Campbell came and we all went to the church to say goodbye to him."

"I know, honey. And he loved you very much. But before I married your daddy, Michael and I…" She was at a loss for words. How did she tell her seven-year-old son that his mom got pregnant and then married someone who wasn't her baby's daddy? The last thing she wanted Conner to think was that he was a mistake.

"Before you were born, me and your mom loved each other and we made a baby. You. But there were a lot of complications and your mom married Zach, and he became your daddy. Does any of this make sense to you?"

"No. None of this makes sense. You're just making this up so you can pretend to be my daddy because you like my mom. That's why you've spent time with me."

"That's not true, Conner. We wanted you to have some time to get to know me better before we told you," Michael said. She could see how Conner's words had hurt him.

"Why don't we go sit down in the living room? Then you can ask all the questions you want to ask and we'll answer them," Devon said, hoping that she could find the right words this time.

"No, I don't want to talk to either of you," Conner said as he turned his tear-filled eyes to her. "You told me we aren't supposed to lie." Then, before Devon could stop him, Conner bolted away and ran out the door.

When she started to go after him, Michael grabbed her arm. "Let him have a moment. He just needs some time to think things through. He's a smart kid."

Devon wasn't sure Michael was right. He'd never seen Conner with Zach. He didn't understand how close the two of them had been, or how hard Zach's death had hit Conner.

"I'll give him a few minutes, then I'll go and check on him. But maybe it's best if you leave before I do that."

"Maybe you're right," Michael said, then leaned down to kiss her. She found herself wanting to pull away, but she didn't understand why. Michael hadn't done anything wrong. It had been her who had kept his son from him. It had been her who had never told her son the truth, though Zach had suggested it several times. And now, she had to fix it all.

She waited until Michael had left, then she went to talk to Conner. She opened the door to his room and found the lights turned out. As she sat down on the bed next to him, she noticed that the pillows were missing off the bed. An uneasiness filled her and she reached down and pulled the covers off Conner. But there was no Conner, only pillows stuffed underneath. She stood and rushed to the light switch, but she already knew what she would find. Conner wasn't in his room.

She rushed through the house, throwing open doors and calling Conner's name. She rushed out the back door, then dashed back inside and out the front door. For a moment, she couldn't remember where she'd left her phone. Then she remembered setting it down on the counter when she and Michael were doing the dishes.

Michael. That had to be it. Conner had to have gone over to Michael's house. It was a couple blocks down the road and she ran all the way. She could see the lights through the windows, then she stopped and took a breath. Conner had been hurt and angry, so he'd come to talk to Michael. She could only hope that Michael would be able to explain things better to Conner than she had been able to. She knocked on the door, then remembered there was a doorbell. She'd just hit the bell when the door opened and Michael stood there staring at her blankly.

She knew immediately that Conner wasn't there.

* * *

"How could he be gone?" Michael asked as he shoved his feet into his tennis shoes.

"I went to check on him, to talk to him about what had happened. I thought he was asleep, but I noticed that there weren't any pillows on the bed. He'd piled them up under the covers to make it look like he was there. He had to have left when I walked you out the front door." Devon followed him down the stairs to the storage room, where all the hurricane preparations were kept.

He pulled out two flashlights and checked them to make sure the batteries were still good. "Okay. So that was only about twenty minutes ago, right? He couldn't have gone far. You didn't see him on your way here—besides, I'm probably the last person that he would come to see."

"I should have driven my car here, then we could have split up." She ran her trembling hands through her hair and Michael knew that she was close to losing it.

"Look, we can't panic. We'll take my truck. We can stop by your house and see if he's come back. If he's not there, I think we should call the police. Then we can drive down to the park. If we don't see him on the road, we'll check the beach. He couldn't have gotten far. Trust me, Devon. We will find him."

They headed for the truck and Michael handed Devon a flashlight as he pulled out of the drive. "Shine it on the sides of the road as we pass. He could be hiding from us. He's probably as scared as we are."

He drove slowly, making sure that he lit up every bush and tree they passed with his flashlight. He stopped once when he thought he saw something move, but it was only a cat exploring the neighborhood.

"Wait, stop. Michael, stop."

"Hold on," he said, then swore when Devon jumped out of the truck before he came to a complete stop. He put the truck in Park, then got out to see what Devon had seen. His heart just about came out of his chest when he circled the back of the truck and saw her bent over something at the side of the road. He'd seen too many patients that had been hit by vehicles and left on the side of the road. His whole body went icy cold with terror.

"This is Conner's bicycle, I'm sure of it," Devon said, standing up and looking around. "But where is he?"

Michael's lungs expanded as he took a deep breath. For a moment, he closed his eyes and said a prayer of thanks. When he opened them, he saw that Devon was walking toward the beach, her light shining on the ground as she walked. "There's footsteps here that look small enough to be his."

As soon as they made it down the path that led to the beach, Devon started calling out for her son. "Conner? Conner, where are you?"

He shone his light to the left and started toward the shoreline while Devon started down the other way. The boy had to be here. Unless…

"Michael, I see him," Devon called.

He turned to see her running down to the shoreline, where the tide was coming in. By the time he caught up to her, he could hear crying. He shone the light out toward the water and saw that Conner was sprawled in the sand, the water rising around him as the tide came in.

After handing his flashlight to Devon, he sprinted through the water until he got to the boy. He started to lift his son into his arms, but when he put his arms under his legs, Conner cried out in pain.

"Conner, what's wrong?" he asked as Devon dropped down beside them.

"I tripped in a hole and hurt my foot," Conner said, lifting his leg up to show them, then whimpering before he reached out his arms to his mom and burst into tears.

"Oh, honey. It's okay. It's all going to be okay. Let's get you home and we can get it checked out. Coach Hart—" Devon shook her head and corrected herself "—I mean, your dad can check to make sure there's nothing broken."

"He's not my dad," Conner shouted, the hurt child suddenly turning into the angry boy Michael had seen earlier.

"We can talk about that later," Michael said. Though Conner's words stung, Michael knew it was a sign that the boy himself was hurting. The life he'd known up until tonight had suddenly changed and been turned upside down. It would take some time for Conner to get used to the changes. "Right now, we need to get you out of these wet clothes and make sure your foot is okay."

"No," Conner protested. "I want to know the truth. I'm not going home until you tell me the truth."

Unsure what to do, the two of them looked at each other, then they both sat down beside their son in the water.

"Okay, I'm going to tell you the whole story now," Devon said. "First, I want to explain that there are two types of fathers. One is called a biological father. Michael is your biological father. And, like he told you, the two of us made a baby and that baby is you. Which is why you have the color of my hair and the color of his eyes. You've got a part of each of us inside you. But there's another kind of father, too. That's what Zach was. He was the father who helped take care of you when you were born. He loved you very much, just as much as if he had made you himself. He was every bit your dad, too. Does that help explain things better?"

Not answering her, Conner turned toward Michael. "But why didn't you take care of me when I was born? Why didn't you come to see me?"

Devon wanted to say that it was all her fault, but before she could, Michael answered him. "Something happened, and me and your mom didn't talk for a long time, not until you came here to live. If I had known that you were my son, I would have come to see you, I promise, but sometimes things happen that we can't change. I can't change that and neither can your mom. But I hope you'll let me see you now. I want to be a good father, but I don't really know how. It sounds like your other dad was a really good one. Maybe you can tell me about him and that will help me do a better job."

"I don't know," Conner said and sniffled, then turned to his mom. "Can I go home now?"

Michael stood and reached down to pick up his son, but Conner turned away from him and reached for his mother.

"No, I've got him," Devon said. Michael took her arm and helped her stand up with her son in her arms.

He started to take Conner from her when she stumbled, but she managed to straighten herself and then tightened her hold on her son. Unable to help himself, he took her arm. Though she didn't pull away, she didn't lean into him, either. It had been a long day and he knew they were all tired, but still it hurt. Badly.

Devon shifted Conner in her arms. Her back and legs strained as they made their way down the path to Michael's truck. Exhaustion was setting in and she had to force her feet to keep moving. All the emotions of the last few hours had drained the life out of her. The pain she'd seen in her son's eyes when she'd tried to explain about his father, the fear of not knowing where he was or if he was safe, then the relief when she'd found him—it had all been too much.

She'd been so foolish to think that she wouldn't have to pay for the decisions she'd made in her life. The last few weeks she'd been so happy, watching Michael and her son spending time together. She'd known that Conner would be confused when she told him about Michael, but she'd never dreamed he'd run away. She should have realized life wasn't that simple. It never had been. Not for her. Even the life she'd built with Zach had always been shadowed by the knowledge that she wasn't being honest with her son. At least that burden had been lifted now.

And Michael? Had she really thought she could have any type of relationship with him without getting emotionally involved? She'd fallen for him when she'd been a teenager and when she'd been a young woman. She should have known she couldn't escape losing her heart to him all over again.

By the time they made it back to her house, Devon knew what she had to do. After she got Conner into some dry pajamas, her son was too tired to complain as Michael examined his foot.

"It looks like you twisted your ankle and sprained it. That means your mom is going to have to put a wrap around it and you're going to have to stay off it for a while," Michael told Conner, though Devon could see that her son was dozing off even as Michael was talking.

"I'll get him into bed and then wrap it," she

said, picking her son off the couch where she'd put him for Michael to examine him. "If it's still swollen tomorrow, I'll take him to get it X-rayed."

"Let me know and I can get the X-ray ordered at work," Michael said, then stood to leave.

"I'll call into work tomorrow and make sure everything is covered, but I'm going to stay home. I need to be with Conner right now." Turning back to her son, she heard the door shut behind her.

CHAPTER FOURTEEN

MICHAEL WALKED OUT the door of what he had once thought was his biggest success. Hart Sports Institute had been the culmination of all his dreams. He'd worked hard to make the surgical center a success with the same tenacity that he'd had for his dream of playing football. In fact, he'd been working toward being an orthopedic doctor and owning a surgical center for sports injuries since the day he'd accepted that his professional football career had ended. He was proud of what he'd accomplished with the surgical center. And he still looked forward to working there with his brother once Matt finished his residency. But for the first time since he'd discovered his talent and love for the game of football, he was able to see that life was about more than just a successful career.

It was about the people in his life. The ones he laughed with and sometimes argued with. The person he wanted to go grocery shopping with or do something as simple as laundry. The person he kissed good-night on the porch and then went home and dreamed of kissing again. After experiencing the last few weeks with Devon and Conner, he felt the loss of those simple, everyday things the most.

As he climbed into his truck, he saw that Devon's car was still in the parking lot. She'd started working later and only arriving in time to pick Conner up from practice. It was just one of the changes she'd made to the routine they'd established before the night they'd told Conner about Michael being his father. Since that night, there had been no invitations to dinner and no visits to Michael's office. Devon was making sure he had no doubt that things between the two of them had changed. Conner's anger at finding out that the father who'd raised him hadn't been his real father had upset both of them, but Michael didn't understand why Devon thought that meant the relationship between him and Devon had to end. Conner's anger would surely subside eventually. Michael had hoped that the two of them showing a united front would have helped him accept the change. But then, what did Michael know? He'd only been a father for a month or so. Maybe Devon had a plan that he didn't understand.

His phone rang over the car system and he answered it after seeing that it was his brother. "Hey, Matt. What's up?"

"Nothing's up here. I'm just living the harried life of a resident. What about you? Any changes in the Conner and Devon situation?" Matt asked.

"No. It's been over a week and she's still doing her best to ignore me." Michael had told Matt everything that had happened the night Conner had run away, leaving out the intimate details of the night before that he and Devon had spent together. "I'm not sure what to do. I don't want to pressure either one of them, but I don't know how much longer I can take this. I feel like Devon and Conner are getting further and further away from me every day."

"So this isn't just about Conner," Matt said, his words a statement instead of a question.

Though Michael hadn't told his brother about the night Devon had slept over, his brother had known that the two of them had gone out together.

"You love her, don't you?" Matt asked.

Michael hadn't said he loved anyone since his parents' death. He loved his brother, but it wasn't something the two of them actually said to each other. But his parents? They'd always told their two sons that they loved them each night at bedtime, and Michael had always told his parents that he loved them. It was one of the first things Michael had missed the first night he'd gone to sleep after they were gone. He would have given anything to have been able to tell them just once more how much he loved them.

But now, there was Devon in his life and, yes, he did love her. Yet, even with everything he'd learned from the loss of his parents, he hadn't been able to say the words. And with her pulling away from him, he might never get the chance.

"What do I know about love? Besides, she's made it plain that she only ever wanted a casual relationship."

"She's protecting her son. She had a bad scare and she's probably feeling a lot of guilt about not telling him earlier. And maybe she's feeling some guilt concerning her husband, too," Matt suggested.

Michael knew that wasn't the problem between the two of them. She'd admitted that he'd badly hurt her all those years ago when he hadn't called her. Was she just as afraid of getting hurt now or messing things up between them as he was?

"I think you do love her, you're just too scared to admit it," Matt said, his voice a bit smug.

"I've hurt her before. I don't want to do that

again," Michael protested. He'd gone through his whole adult life without ever thinking about falling in love. The closest he had ever felt had been that night he'd spent with… Devon. What if that was it? What if the reason he'd never fallen in love with anyone else was because he'd never felt anything that compared to that night all those years ago with Devon? Not the sex, or at least not just the sex. But the way they'd laughed and talked. He had been so happy with her that night. Just like he had that night on the cruise. And the next morning, when he'd woken up with her by his side? He'd never felt anything like that level of happiness before.

Michael turned into the sports complex and parked. He looked over and saw Conner sitting on one of the benches at the side of the field.

"If you love her, you won't hurt her. You've had enough losses in your life, Mickey, and you've fought for every win you've had. Don't stop fighting now."

Michael sat in the truck for a few minutes after he and Matt ended their call. His brother was right. He'd lost a lot in his life, but he'd never just given up. Now, the most important thing in his life, a life with Devon and Conner, was right there in front of him. He had never been one to stand on the sidelines. He'd always fought his way into the game. That had been the key to his success. So maybe it was time for him to get off those sidelines and start fighting for the life he wanted so badly.

Making a decision that he hoped he wouldn't regret, he walked over to where Conner was putting on his cleats. Michael had stayed away from the practice field until today, giving Bryan the excuse of work while actually not wanting to cause Conner any further distress. He was now starting to believe that it had been a mistake not to be around Conner. What if his son thought he was mad at him or, even worse, that he didn't want to be troubled with an angry little boy?

"Hey, Conner," Michael said, coming up behind him as he worked on tying his shoestrings.

"Hey, Coach Hart," Conner said. The boy looked up at him and for a moment Michael would have sworn that his son was happy to see him. Then, as if Conner remembered that he was supposed to be mad at Michael, his smile disappeared and his eyes dropped down.

Michael took a seat next to his son. "I don't know about you, but I'm feeling really confused and sad right now."

"You are?" Conner asked, looking up at him. "Why?"

"I guess I'm confused about what is going

on between you and me and your mother," Michael said, deciding to just be honest with the little boy. "And I'm sad because I miss spending time with the two of you. I thought that we were friends."

"I thought so, too, but you were just coming around because you're one of my dads," Conner said, his words as sad-sounding as Michael's.

"Now, that's where you're wrong. I liked hanging out with you. I'll admit that I think it's great having a son like you. I'm very proud of you. And I love the way you aren't afraid to ask questions about things you don't understand. I wish that I could tell your other dad how much I appreciate him for the way he raised you."

"You do?" Conner asked, sitting up straight now.

"I definitely do. Your mom has told me about what a great dad he was and I'm so glad you had him in your life."

"But why weren't you there? I still don't understand how you didn't know about me," Conner said.

"When your mama found out she was going to have you, she was very happy. But when she called to tell me about it, I was in the hospital. I had been really badly hurt playing football and I was all broken up."

"I know," Max said, "you had a broken arm and a broken leg and some other stuff too. She said that was why you quit football." There was no sign of the anger Conner had shown earlier. He was interested in Michael's story now. Michael only hoped that it would help Conner understand things better.

"I had a lot of injuries and my head hurt, too. I was in the hospital for a long time and it made it hard for your mom to get in touch with me. Your mom did try, though. But when she couldn't, she decided that she wanted you to have a father. So she and your father, Zach, got married. They were so happy when you were born. Then your dad got sick and had to leave you."

"I still miss him," Conner whispered. "Even if you're my dad, too, I still love him."

"Of course you love him. I want you to love him. He was a great dad." Michael saw a tear run down his son's face and he couldn't help but put his arm around him. When Conner didn't shy away from him, he pulled him closer into his side. "Conner, I will never stand in the way of you loving your first father."

"My first father?" Conner asked, sniffling against Michael's side.

"Yes, he was your first dad, right?" Michael would always regret that he had missed his son's first words, first steps, and every other first up until now, but he felt no bitterness toward the man who'd been there beside Conner for them.

"Yeah," Conner agreed. "So you're my second dad, then?"

Michael sat and thought for a moment. Having Conner call him dad at all would be wonderful. "I guess I am. Now, can I ask you a question?"

"Sure," Conner replied. "What is it?"

"What would you think if I told you that I love both you and your mother? Would that be okay with you?"

"Are you going to marry her?" Conner's sudden crooked smile couldn't have gotten any wider and it was like the sun coming out on a cold day. "Then you'll be my stepdad, too."

"You'd be okay with me marrying your mom?" Michael asked.

Conner nodded enthusiastically.

"Why such a hurry? I'm not sure she wants to see me right now. And she might not want to marry me." His stomach twisted with the thought that his son could be wrong and Devon might turn him down. She'd said that she didn't trust easily and he'd already hurt her badly once. What if she was afraid to give him a chance? Or, worse, what if she didn't feel the same about him as he felt about her?

"But you told me that you have to ask a question if you want to know the answer. Besides, she's been crying every night after I go to bed. She thinks I don't hear her, but I do." Conner stood and took hold of Michael's hand and began pulling at him.

"Your mother's crying?" Michael said, letting Conner help pull him off the bench. He didn't like the idea of Devon crying.

"I think it's because I got mad and made you go away. It makes me feel real sad. She's at work so you just need to go find her and ask her to marry you. Then you'll be my second dad and my mom will be happy."

"It's not your fault, Conner. Your mom is just worried about doing the right thing for you." Michael thought about what his son had said. It seemed all three of them were miserable with the way things were now. As a plan began to form in his mind, he turned to Conner. "What do you say the two of us find a way to fix this?"

Devon walked down the beach gathering the shells that her son had insisted he needed right then. It had been a long day at work and she didn't feel like taking a walk on the beach, but today was the first day she had seen any excitement in her son's eyes since the night he'd learned about Michael being his father and she wasn't about to disappoint him.

She bent over to where a group of shells had washed up and began to go through them, looking for the perfect shell. Standing up again, she looked around for Conner and began to panic until she saw him several yards ahead of her. But he wasn't alone.

She stood there, unable to move, as Michael walked toward her. Even with all the injuries he had suffered, he still moved with the grace of an athlete. She'd missed him so much that she'd cried herself to sleep each night. She'd messed up everything between them. First, she'd let things go too far with him. She should have known that once she was in his arms she could never stop herself from falling for him all over again. Now, she had to find some excuse for why she couldn't see him anymore. Not like that. And then there was Conner. She'd made such a mess of that, too. Her son was so angry with Michael and none of it was Michael's fault. It was hers. She was the one who had kept Conner from his father.

"Hi, Sunshine," Michael said as he joined her.

"Hi, Mickey. Is everything okay with Conner?" She hoped the fact that her son had gone to Michael was a good sign that he was getting over some of his anger.

"Conner and I are good. He helped me plan this," Michael said, his eyes heavy with a look of longing that she knew would pull her in if she wasn't careful.

"Plan?" she asked, confused. "What plan?"

"Well, the two of us were talking and he reminded me that if you don't ask a question you'll never know the answer. And since I wasn't sure how I could get you to talk to me since you've been avoiding me, I got him to help me get you here."

"So the two of you have a question for me?" She was reminded of the time when she had been sure that he was going to ask her to marry him. That time it had turned out to be an invitation to a football game, but there was no telling what the two of them had in mind now. Not that she cared. The fact that Conner was talking to Michael was a good step forward.

"No, I'm the one with the question. Conner is here for moral support." Michael looked back to where their son still stood several yards away from them.

"Okay, I'm ready. What is it?" she asked. She didn't know how much longer she could stand there when all she wanted to do was throw herself into his arms. It had been so hard for her to stay away from him for the last week, but she knew now that it was better that she stop things between them before they went any further.

"It's very simple really. I've spent all my life working to make some dream of mine come true and now, I know that no matter how successful I am, without you and Conner in my life I'll never be happy. I want you both in my life forever. I haven't had time to get a ring, so I can't do this the right way yet, but I have to know now. Sunshine, will you marry me?"

Her eyes shot to his and her heart began to pound. Michael wanted to marry her? But was he just doing this for their son? It was like history repeating itself again. She'd married Zach and never regretted it. But this time there was a difference. This time she was in love and she didn't think she could be happy in a marriage with Michael where that love wasn't returned.

"You don't have to make a decision right now. You can take your time. I just can't go on with things the way they are now. I love you so much and I'm miserable without you."

Something broke inside of Devon hearing Michael's words. She tried to hold back the tears, but couldn't. "You really love me?"

"Of course I love you. I think I always have,"

Michael said. "I've spent my whole life chasing my dreams. First, it was football and then it was medical school. Then it was setting up a practice and building this place. But the last few days I've discovered that none of it matters. It's you who matters. This feeling I have for you, it's more than I've ever felt for anything or anyone in my life, because you've become my whole life. You're all I want. You and Conner. I just need to know if you feel the same way about me."

Devon brushed at the tears rolling down her cheeks, then placed her wet hands against Michael's cheeks. "Yes, I do. I love you and I always have. And, yes, I will marry you."

EPILOGUE

DEVON LOOKED DOWN from the balcony to the party taking place on the beach below her. It was supposed to have been a small wedding. A few family members, a few coworkers, and a few close friends were all that had been expected. But when word had gotten out that the hometown football hero and the granddaughter of one of Silver Sands's dearly loved residents were getting married, the invitation list had grown, and the whole beach in front of Michael's home was filled with guests dancing in the sand with the stars and moon shining high above them.

"I can't believe they're all still here," Michael said as he came up behind her, slipping his arms around her.

"I can't, either," she said, leaning back against him. The wedding had been over for hours now. The cake had been cut and eaten, the toasts given. The live band that had been hired for the reception had been gone for at least an hour.

She suspected that it had been Matt who had turned on the outside speakers and was streaming music through them. She also suspected that the woman he was now dancing with was the reason why. "Who is that woman Matt's dancing with? I can't quite see from here."

Michael leaned over her and began to laugh. "That's Rachel."

"Our Rachel?" Devon asked, stunned that the beautiful woman dancing below them could be the same one who worked as one of the surgical representatives that assisted in their operating rooms. Devon had to admit that she'd never seen Rachel out of scrubs, but the difference from how she looked at work was startling.

"I almost didn't recognize her myself. I hope Matt doesn't go falling for her," Michael said thoughtfully.

"Why? They're both single and she's always seemed very kind and levelheaded." Devon knew that Michael was protective of his brother, but what harm could come from Matt having a little romance in his life?

"She has a reputation of being a little wary where men are concerned," Michael said.

"Well, she doesn't seem to be that way right now," Devon said as she watched the woman wrapping her arms around Matt's neck as they danced off away from the rest of the crowd.

"Hmm," Michael said, his breath warm against her neck as his lips began to move downward.

Leaning back into his body, she glanced up at the stars above them. Their wedding day had been perfect. And with Conner happily going off to spend a few days at Max's house, they had the nights to themselves for a while.

"Come inside," Michael urged, taking her hand to lead her inside.

"But there's still people here. What will they think if we leave them?" She didn't want to be rude to everyone who'd come to celebrate with them.

"They'll think I'm a very lucky man," Michael laughed as he turned her in his arms.

Devon looked up at her husband and her heart had never felt so full. "I love you, Mickey."

"And I will always love you, my Sunshine." Michael said, before leaning down and kissing her lips.

* * * * *

Look out for the next story in the Sunshine State Surgeons duet

Coming soon!

And if you enjoyed this story, check out these other great reads from Deanne Anders

Festive Reunion with the Doctor
Single Dad's Fake Fiancée
The Rebel Doctor's Secret Child
Unbuttoning the Bachelor Doc

All available now!

Get up to 4 Free Books!

We'll send you 2 free books from each series you try PLUS a free Mystery Gift.

Both the **Harlequin Presents** and **Harlequin Medical Romance** series feature exciting stories of passion and drama.

YES! Please send me 2 FREE novels from Harlequin Presents or Harlequin Medical Romance and my FREE gift (gift is worth about $10 retail). I may cancel anytime by emailing ReaderServiceInfo@Harlequin.com or by calling 1-800-873-8635.If I don't cancel, I will receive 6 brand-new larger-print novels every month and be billed just $7.19 each in the U.S., or $7.99 each in Canada, or 4 brand-new Harlequin Medical Romance Larger-Print books every month and be billed just $7.19 each in the U.S. or $7.99 each in Canada. That's a savings of 20% off the cover price! It's quite a bargain! Shipping and handling is just 75¢ per book in the U.S. and $1.75 per book in Canada.* I understand that accepting the free books and gift places me under no obligation to buy anything—they are mine to keep for free no matter what I decide.

Choose one: ☐ **Harlequin Presents Larger-Print** (176/376 BPA G3CD) ☐ **Harlequin Medical Romance** (171/371 BPA G3CD) ☐ **Or Try Both!** (176/376 & 171/371 BPA G3CE)

Name (please print)

Address Apt. #

City State/Province Zip/Postal Code

Email: Please check this box ☐ if you would like to receive newsletters and promotional emails from Harlequin Enterprises ULC and its affiliates. You can unsubscribe anytime.

Mail to the **Harlequin Reader Service:**
IN U.S.A.: P.O. Box 1341, Buffalo, NY 14240-8531
IN CANADA: P.O. Box 603, Fort Erie, Ontario L2A 5X3

Want to explore our other series or interested in ebooks? Visit www.ReaderService.com or call 1-800-873-8635.

*Terms and prices subject to change without notice. Prices do not include sales taxes, which will be charged (if applicable) based on your state or country of residence. Canadian residents will be charged applicable taxes. Offer not valid in Quebec. This offer is limited to one order per household. Books received may not be as shown. Not valid for current subscribers to the Harlequin Presents or Harlequin Medical Romance series. All orders subject to approval. Credit or debit balances in a customer's account(s) may be offset by any other outstanding balance owed by or to the customer. Please allow 4 to 6 weeks for delivery. Offer available while quantities last.

Your Privacy — Your information is being collected by Harlequin Enterprises ULC, operating as Harlequin Reader Service. For a complete summary of the information we collect, how we use this information and to whom it is disclosed, please visit our privacy notice located at https://corporate.harlequin.com/privacy-notice. Notice to California Residents—Under California law, you have specific rights to control and access your data. For more information on these rights and how to exercise them, visit https://corporate.harlequin.com/california-privacy. For additional information for residents of other U.S. states that provide their residents with certain rights with respect to personal data, visit https://corporate.harlequin.com/other-state-residents-privacy-rights.

HPHM2603